BAILEY THOMAS

Kane's Reckoning

MILL CREEK MYSTIQUE
BOOK 4

BTA PUBLISHING

Published by BTA Publishing

Cover Design: Melody Pond

melodyypond.weebly.com

Interior Design: A Fabulous Production

afabulousproduction.com

This is a work of fiction. The characters, incidents, and dialogues in this book are of the author's imagination and are not to be construed as real. Any resemblance to actual events or persons, living or dead, is completely coincidental.

PAPERBACK ISBN: 978-1-967156-12-2 EBOOK ISBN: 978-1-967156-11-5

First Edition: May 2026

MILL CREEK MYSTIQUE SERIES

A collection of stand alone, small town, romantic suspense novels. Each book can be read independently but features characters from the town of Mill Creek.

Suggested Reading Order

Trent's Redemption

Hidden Identities

Breaking Point

Kane's Reckoning

Legally Bound - Coming Soon

Author's Note

Kane's Reckoning was originally slated to be the first book in my Mill Creek Mystique series, a town inspired by a place where I spent summers with my family. Ultimately, my publisher decided that this story wouldn't be the first book in the series and set it aside for *Trent's Redemption*, my debut novel.

While the mining elements are not the main focus of *Kane's Reckoning*, all the mining details in this story are nods to my father, a humble miner. At the time that I interviewed him as part of the research and planning stages of this story, he was living with Parkinson's disease, which limited everything he loved doing, both cognitively and physically. Finding common ground for engagement became increasingly difficult, but when he talked about mining, he traveled back in time and found some happiness. Even though I knew that not every story or detail would make it into the story, it allowed him to contribute. He had a purpose, and it was clear in every conversation how proud he was of his history.

Unfortunately, my father passed away just before *Trent's Redemption* was published, which broke my heart. Continuing the Mill Creek Mystique series with *Kane's Reckoning* became very difficult to write. I had tried countless times to keep working on it, but my heart wasn't ready. The stack of notes from my interviews, every page I reviewed and revised, brought me back to my dad's room and all those conversations where he became part of its fabric.

Finally, I'm ready to share Kane and Annika's story, which is set just before the start of the events in *Trent's Redemption*. Since this series is standalone, you can read these books in any order.

Hold on to those you love, tell them you love them often, and cherish beautiful memories of the time spent with them.

XOXO,

Bailey

Contents

To my ride-or-die, who lives by the motto that you should never desert dessert. I love you to the moon and back!

To my father, we did it! Better late than never.

In loving memory of Danny, who had a golden heart and a warm smile, you will be deeply missed.

One

January—Current Day

Mill Creek

Annika Bauer had survived.

Joyfulness surged through her, giving way to an eagerness to begin this new year. From her porch, she inhaled the frosty morning air. Crystals from the latest snowfall dotted the once-grassy meadow, while rays of light danced, creating a spectrum of color with the rising sun.

She loved it here.

From behind her, Kane slid his strong arms around her middle, securing her against his firm chest. There wasn't a better feeling in the world than being wrapped up in her husband's embrace. Safe. Loved. Happy.

"Morning, sweetheart," he whispered against her ear. "Are you warm enough in your pajamas and robe?"

She nestled into his body, loving how his heat warmed her backside. "Have I told you how much I love our home?"

"A few times, but my ego loves it every time you do," he replied. His deep voice rumbled just above her, adding another layer of comfort.

She sighed. "It's a shame your family never appreciated your architectural talent."

"They didn't appreciate a good many things," he said, a puff of condensation following each word. Kane twisted her frame around until he could cup her cheeks. "It still haunts me knowing that I almost lost you."

She rested her head against his chest, hugging him like a breeze might push them apart. The fuzzy softness of his cashmere sweater caressed her cheek. They stood connected for a few minutes. She'd found contentment in this simple pleasure. A haven she cherished.

"I almost lost you, too."

She never wanted to return to that level of fear or anxiety. Today, she would stop hiding from the pain and the truth of what she endured. It was time to share her story with her friends, whom she adored.

Unable to spare any more minutes, she lifted her head to raise up on her tiptoes to kiss Kane's lips. "If we don't get moving, I'll be late for brunch. I volunteered to bring the leftover champagne from our New Year's Eve party."

Kane gifted her with one of his signature male-model smiles, which melted her insides. "Do you want to take both cases?"

"No, silly, that's too much! One case will work," she replied, grasping his hand and nudging him toward the house—the better to admire the view of his backside, his tailored slacks molding perfectly to his toned body.

Kane paused at the granite countertop in the kitchen, swiping his keys off the counter. "Go get ready. I'll load the champagne into the Range Rover," he said.

"Thank you," she replied.

She padded down the hallway toward their master suite, then paused. "Hey, Kane, don't forget your new baseball glove. I put it on the workbench in the garage."

"Got it," he groused. "Eat something scrumptious for me because I'll be cold, hungry, and wearing the worst pants ever made while playing ball with the guys."

She burst into giggles. "Clarke would die from laughter if he heard you complaining. It's a league, Kane. You signed up for this with everyone, remember?"

"Yeah, I'm aware, but I don't remember being forewarned about the uniform. Whoever designed an outfit made entirely of polyester should be banned from designing clothing," Kane groaned.

Annika laughed harder as she continued down the hallway. She had come to accept that she married a man of fashion, but she'd never give up trying to bring a bit of denim and casual style into his life. "Think of it as an adventure, Kane. You're doing something you missed out on."

She loved that man more than her next breath. Kane may have lived a life of privilege she couldn't imagine until recently, but there was so much childhood he didn't get a chance to experience—his first pair of cutoff shorts, making mud pies, playing ball with the boys.

Annika stepped into her steamy shower, rushing to get ready. If she were late, she would never hear the end of it from Aimee. She swore that girl was becoming more like Clarke every day. That thought made her grin. She slid behind the steering wheel, enjoying the buttery-soft leather as it molded to her body. Once the engine roared to life, she hit the seat warmer button. Whoever had invented that feature would hold a place in her heart forever.

Before long, she was pulling into her friend's driveway. The front door opened, revealing three smiling women rushing to hug her. Maggie was hosting the brunch, although she was still learning to cook. Thankfully, Aimee brought the lion's share of the food. Jasmine was joining them today, too; she and Noah were back in town from the holidays.

"Finally! I thought you and Kane got tangled in the tinsel," Aimee said.

"Did you bring the champagne?" Maggie asked at the same time.

"Aimee, I'm like thirty seconds late," Annika replied. She pressed the button to lift the tailgate. "In the back, Maggie."

"It's good to see you, Annika," Jasmine called over the chatter.

Yes, these were her girls, Annika thought warmly. She loved them dearly and loved spending time with them. She followed everyone inside into the kitchen, where they settled into a comfortable chorus of activity as though they had done these types of gatherings their entire lives, not a matter of months.

A loud pop echoed as Jamine opened the champagne. She poured some into each flute with a splash of orange juice before distributing them. "Ladies, to us! May good health, lots of laughter, and zero calories or wrinkles follow us into the new year!

The clinking of glasses and murmurs of approval followed.

"I'm guessing not pregnant?" Annika asked Maggie, as her friend sipped her mimosa.

"No, it was a damn false positive. However, Trent was adorable, taking the blame and declaring that we need to double our baby-making time."

After a moment, she rested her head on Annika's shoulder. "The doctor said when the time was right, it would happen. I just want it to happen sooner rather than later, you know."

Aimee took a drink of her own bubbly concoction. "I'm all for being Auntie Aimee, Maggie. Don't worry; we'll be throwing you a baby shower in no time."

Maggie lifted her head and smiled. "So, Aimee, any wedding plans yet?"

Aimee slipped on two oven mitts to place the quiche on a trivet to cool, the buttery pastry scenting the air. "No, we're enjoying the whole engagement period. I want to make sure that whatever we decide, it works for Clarke's aunt to attend."

Annika pointed the pie server at Aimee. "Remember Maggie's wedding in front of the old mill last fall? It was stunning. All the bright leaves against her white dress—she looked magical."

Jasmine's brows popped up excitedly. "That's a great idea! It would also be familiar ground for Clarke's aunt."

"You're right—I'll have to run that past the big guy," Aimee nodded. "Quiche is ready, ladies."

Another round of cheers filled the room as everyone started serving themselves.

"I'm starving and so thankful that Aimee cooked for us," Annika said as she elbowed Maggie. "That fruit salad looks amazing. Did you make that, Maggie?"

Maggie harrumphed and said, "Yes, I made it all from scratch, right down to chopping all of it. Isn't it a masterpiece?"

Annika, Aimee, and Jasmine burst into laughter. They headed toward the living room, where the sound of forks scraping against ceramic followed. Annika loved how everyone fit together—a shared understanding. Whether they were shopping, eating, or just sitting in silence, this group clicked. The fact that they were all survivors may have brought them together, but the friendship they forged made them a sisterhood.

"Man, this fruit salad is out of this world! You'll have to get me the recipe, Maggie," Annika said, winking at Maggie's playfully annoyed face.

"One day, ladies, I'm going to cook a meal that will rival this one." Maggie retorted.

"Aimee, next time you make a quiche, make an extra so I can have one," Annika said.

Maggie rolled her eyes at Annika before mumbling around a mouthful of food, "Make it three."

"This is delicious! Make it four," Jasmine piped up. "I know I'm the newest to this sisterhood, but you all are the best. And so damn fierce. Just thinking about what we all endured is humbling."

Aimee laughed and patted Jasmine's shoulder, then placed her empty plate on the coffee table.

Annika added her plate to the stack. "I love that we have this big extended family vibe happening. I think it's amazing that someday our children will get to grow up with each other."

"How did you and Kane get together? I know something went down, but I don't know the details."

The room went still. Aimee and Maggie paused as their gazes traveled between Jasmine and Annika.

"Shoot, did I say something wrong?" Jasmine frowned with concern.

"No," Maggie said, flashing Jasmine a small, comforting smile. "It's just that Annika has never shared her story with any of us. Well, we know the gist of it, but not the whole of it."

Aimee leaned forward to grab her flute. "There's no pressure, but if you're ready to share, we'd like to hear it."

Annika froze as a sudden rush of panic washed over her. This was exactly what she had wanted to do today during brunch. And she *was* ready to tell her story. She just needed a moment to gather her composure.

"It's okay, Annika, another time." Aimee shifted her attention away from Annika. "So, Jasmine—"

"No, I'm ready. It's past time, but I'll warn you, it's a long story."

Without a word, Aimee, Jasmine, and Maggie enveloped her in hugs. She was humbled by the power of their love and support. These women were part of her family.

"Don't you leave out one detail, Annika," Maggie said, right before hugging her again.

Once everyone returned to their seats, Annika started. "Let's start when I first met Kane, right before you came to Trent for help, Maggie."

Two

June—Six Months Earlier

New York City

Annika looked at her alarm clock again and groaned. The number eleven stared back at her, making her feel like Monday would never end. The endless nights were the hardest to endure; her demons were always louder and more persistent after sunset. In the blanketing darkness, it was hard to ignore the ugly memories she preferred to keep buried.

Now, she'd have to wait until the sun peeked over the horizon, dancing between skyscrapers, for her monster to retreat. She blew out a frustrated breath. She reached up and lightly touched the soft, puffy skin under her eyes, knowing it would be ringed with dark smudges.

Adapting to the pace and newness of New York City added another layer of change to Annika's healing process. A fresh start and new perspective made sense. Her therapist agreed, though she cautioned Annika that such a big change could stir up a pot of emotions. While her decision to move from Los Angeles was the right choice, the hardest part of her self-induced relocation was realizing her fear and pain still followed her. She knew moving wouldn't erase her history, but she had hoped it would at least quiet it.

Her parents were supportive of her move, but she knew deep down they didn't like it. Her trauma was hers, but they had experienced it from a different angle. Still, they swallowed their fear, realizing they couldn't shield her from everything.

She huffed out another breath and stretched her body to grab the television remote from the side table. This tiny, Midtown studio cost her more than her two-bedroom apartment in LA, which had included parking and a view. However, she saw the appeal of giving up square footage to live in the heart of New York City. It would be impossible to become bored with so much to do, see, and eat on any given day. But what appealed to her most was the anonymity of being one of many who traveled the streets daily.

Her mind shifted back to the goal of the moment: to fill her head with enough trivial nonsense long enough to fall asleep. A full night of peaceful slumber sounded marvelous, and she would need it to be her best for the job interview tomorrow. She plumped up her pillows and snuggled down into the futon. She fumbled with the up and down buttons on the remote, searching through the channels until she found something upbeat to watch. Seconds turned into minutes before she finally drifted off to sleep.

A loud bang and the distinct sound of splintering wood jarred Annika awake. A tremor wracked her body, immobilizing her as she strained to hear what came next.

How had he found her?

Her heart thundered in her chest. It was hard to hear over the rush of blood running through her body. Desperately, she tried to scream, but only a pathetic squeak escaped her throat. She was going to die, and there was no one else around to stop it from happening.

A dark figure stood by her door, here to finish what he had started, but all she could do was stare at his silhouette.

No, damnit! She was tired of being a victim. She hadn't come this far to give up now.

Sucking down a sharp, deep breath, she centered all of her strength to scramble off the bed. Her limbs were heavy and leaden, making her movements clumsy, but she wrestled with the sheets and pillows until the cold and hard wall pressed against her back. Her eyes darted across the small space, trying to locate her attacker. Where was he?

She blinked her eyes several times, her chest heaving as she struggled to calm her breath. Flickers of light from the television illuminated the room, a commercial playing on the screen. Shadows marred the items in her apartment, giving her kitchenette an eerie appearance.

As she worked to process what she thought she saw, the ominous images of her studio faded. Her door remained intact, hanging from its hinges with the chain lock engaged. There was no one by the door—only a hat stand from which a coat hung, the gloomy darkness making it look larger and somewhat human. She was utterly alone, but very much alive.

Her panic dissolved along with her remaining strength. Exhaustion and frustration claimed her as she slid down the wall. When she reached the floor, she buried her face in her hands and sobbed burning, hot tears.

The moment she'd walked into her therapist's office, winning this battle to heal became non-negotiable. This nightmare consumed her. How could she dare to live in the present, dream of a future, when her past tainted every damn thing? She wanted herself back, not this silhouette of who she used to be.

She shook her head to clear her mind, needing to hear the two voices that gave her strength and surrounded her with love. She found her phone on the nightstand and dialed the number she knew by heart.

"Hey, Mom."

"Hi, sweetheart. Are you okay? It's late," her mom asked, jumping right to the point of the call.

Annika closed her eyes and swallowed. "Everything is fine."

Her mom paused. Her concern was evident, but she didn't press the point. Instead, she launched into a full lineup of questions. "How's city life? Have you met any new people?"

She pictured her mom sitting on their sofa, waving to her father to join the conversation. The last thing Annika wanted to do was validate her mother's concern. She pulled at a strand of hair and twirled it around her finger. "Not really, I'm not feeling that social yet. I'm still learning my way around town. There is so much to do here; I can't wait for you to visit."

The East Coast lifestyle and the sheer density of people and cultures present in this magnificent city were awe-inspiring. Even learning how to tackle daily tasks took different considerations, like deciding between walking, riding the subway, or hailing a cab. Although the choice to walk seemed to be her last option, at some point, she had to get used to walking the streets. If not, that creep won.

"Sweetheart, this move won't accomplish your goals if you don't put yourself out there and start taking baby steps," her mother said, her voice firm but laced with a mother's love.

"I know, Mom, but that's easier said than done. I do have some good news—I have an interview tomorrow for a short-term nannying position."

"Oh, that's wonderful, dear! We can't wait to hear all about it."

Annika heard the muted sounds of the phone being passed off to her father.

"Sweet girl, did you get the card we sent you?"

"Yes, Dad. Thanks for the extra money."

Annika heard her mother's raised voice in the background as she began braiding a large section of her hair. "Don't laugh when you hear his idea."

"Ignore your mother. This is a great idea. The fifty-dollar bill is for your sock. Pickpocketing and purse snatching can be common in big cities. If you fold the bill into quarters and place it inside your sock, you'll always have money to get home safely."

Annika heard her mother giggling in the background as the side of her mouth ticked up. Her father looked out for those he loved. She couldn't help but poke him a little. "What if I'm wearing sandals, Dad?"

"Nope, you should only wear sneakers and socks. They provide better foot protection and overall support."

She heard another exchange before her mother was back on the line. "Sweetheart, put the money in your bra."

Annika laughed wholeheartedly. She could almost hear her father's distress through the line at the mere mention of female undergarments. No doubt he was several shades of red by now. She unraveled her braid while listening to her parents' side conversation. Their love was clearly reflected in almost everything they did. Would she ever find her perfect match?

Interrupting their banter, Annika chimed in. "Okay, I've got it. I can store my fifty in many places. I gotta go, but I love you both. And yes, I'll be careful."

"We love you too, sweet girl. We'll talk soon," her father said as her mother shouted from the background, "Call us when you hear from the nanny agency! Love you!"

When the call ended, she noted she was already feeling better; warmth suffused her body. She desperately wanted structure to her days, and a job would check that box. She hoped this assignment from the agency would be a good fit. She would be traveling to Idaho with her charge for an extended period while her employer stayed in London for business.

Nancy, one of the agency's managing administrators, had told her that the Millers had been clients of the agency for nearly fifty years. When a routine background check had brought Annika's past to the forefront, Nancy had every right to ask deeper questions, given how high-profile the clients were. While difficult, Annika knew there was nothing to hide, so she shared what she'd endured in dealing with her stalker in Los Angeles.

Before her ordeal, her goal had been to open a private practice to help children through life's difficulties. Now, that goal, and any plans to start her Masters in Psychology program, were on the back burner. She couldn't even think about providing therapy until she'd put her demons to rest...if she was ever able to.

Kane Miller loved flying into LaGuardia Airport because his flights always included a private architectural tour of New York City. Whether it was daytime or nighttime, his soul and passion were recharged every time he took in the magnificent views of the city. Architecture was his love language. From drafting his visions to constructing his masterpieces, he took pride in how he would leave his mark on the world. Maybe, if his wildest dream came true, his designs would one day be studied around the world. No feeling felt more powerful for him. *Except in knowing this irritates my father to no end.*

As he exited the private terminal, he saw his chauffeur waiting outside for him near his Bentley. Albert grinned widely as Kane approached. "Welcome back, Mr. Miller. As always, it's a pleasure to see you. I trust you had a good trip?"

Kane rolled his eyes at Albert's formal greeting as he slid into the backseat of the SUV. Once the older man shut the driver's door, he leaned forward to talk to him face-to-face. "You know to call me Kane."

"I know. But in public, I'm your employee. It's a matter of respect," Albert said as the vehicle moved forward.

Kane and his older brother Craig had grown up spending most of their time being escorted and driven around New York City by Albert. At some point, Albert and Linda had become their surrogate grandparents, a distinction he and his brother had kept to themselves. While their parents were never present for anything except milestone events, Albert and his wife Linda enthusiastically attended most of their school and extracurricular events, cameras always in their hands.

He still had the scrapbooks, or brag books as Linda called them, that she had made for each of them over the years, detailing every big moment. He was always touched by the meaning and love behind that book.

His own mother had only had professional photographers take portraits of his family every so often. Any other significant event covered in the local society magazines or newspapers was displayed on the coffee table for a limited time.

"Albert, you're family. You've earned that right years ago." Kane said, patting his shoulder to emphasize his meaning.

Albert nodded before shifting back into chauffeur mode. "Do you need to stop anywhere on the way home?"

"Nope. Just home to KPM Towers." He sighed wistfully, thinking of the building he designed himself. "I don't know if I'll ever grow tired of seeing it."

"She's a beauty," Albert agreed.

"I could design and build a lean-to, and both you and Linda would be proud."

"You bet we would. Linda wouldn't live in it, but she'd gush all the same. She loves to snack on all those fancy little appetizers and to tell all of Manhattan about you," Albert replied merrily as he turned onto the Parkway.

Kane's chest warmed at those words. As the patriarch of the family, the mighty Bruce Miller's philosophy on feelings and overt affection meant that those things made a person weak and open to exploitation and manipulation. Everyone and everything was a means to an end, and that endgame always served Bruce's interests.

However, under Albert and Linda's care, he and his brother had learned what unconditional love and unwavering support meant. They could always count on the couple, no matter what. It was those life lessons that had changed something fundamental within him, propelling him to pursue his dreams of architecture, a decision that put him and his father directly at odds most of the time.

Bruce Miller had different paths planned out for his sons.

As they drew near KPM Towers, Kane soaked in the view as if it were his first time seeing it. This was his purpose and the love of his life. Happiness bubbled inside of him, making him eager to move on to his next project.

A few moments later, his vehicle came to a stop. As the doorman opened his door and started retrieving his baggage from the trunk, Kane leaned forward again. "Thanks, Albert. Give my love to Linda."

He thumped the roof to signal he was clear before following the doorman into his building and up to his unit. His cell phone rang. When he recognized the caller, he smiled and picked up.

"Hey, big brother, you have impeccable timing. I just got home from Alaska."

"I know." Craig's voice was tight and clipped. "I need your help."

Kane stopped flipping through the mail he'd retrieved from the main desk. Everything around him faded away as he zeroed in on that one small sentence his brother uttered. He couldn't remember the last time Craig had called him for help. His brother always had everything under control.

At his front door, he took a twenty-dollar bill from his billfold and handed it to the doorman, gesturing that Kane would get it from here. Once his luggage was stowed in the foyer, he returned his undivided attention to the phone. "Absolutely, what's up?"

"It's complicated, but the bottom line is that I need to send Leah home early from London," Craig explained. "The Warwick Mine, which the company purchased, has attracted considerable negative attention from locals, the media, and environmentalist groups, including Global Peace and Harmony. There have been riots, vandalism, and now it's escalated to attacks right outside our home. Last night was the worst of it so far. Someone threw a Molotov cocktail at my vehicle as we pulled into the parking garage."

"Shit, Craig, were you hurt?"

"No. Luckily, it sailed over the car and smashed into the pillar next to us, but Leah was pretty scared."

"Have you expanded your own security protection?" Kane asked.

"Sort of, but in the end, I'm not worried about myself." Kane was not sure what *sort of* meant, but he also knew now was not the time to press. Craig went on to say, "Leah may be too young to understand all of this, but I won't tolerate her being placed in any danger. It's time to send her to New York so she's not here to witness any more of this escalation."

"Understood. When do you need me to pick up Madison and Leah at the airport?"

"Madison and I are still finalizing the arrangements, but very soon. I don't want Leah to stay with Mom and Dad, so I'm sending her to stay with you. Plus, you're her favorite uncle."

"Uh, I'm fairly certain I'm her only one."

"However, I need Madison's help to wrap up this project, so she'll come back to London right away," Craig added. "We won't be back until the end of June at the latest."

Kane's mind exploded with questions. That was roughly a month away. He loved Leah to pieces and would never let his brother down, but the idea of caring for her scared the shit out of him.

"I'm planning to hire a nanny to assist while Leah is with you, since I can already hear you sorting out your whole *I'm-a-bachelor-taking-care-of-a-child* situation," Craig teased.

"I appreciate it, brother, but how hard can taking care of a six-year-old be?"

Craig's laughter helped release some tension. "I'll remind you of that statement after she's been with you a few days. You will be amazed at how much energy or how many never-ending questions she has.

I figured joining you in Idaho while you visit Trent will be a great experience for her. You always enjoyed going out there."

Choosing to ignore him, Kane typed out a text to Trent, confirming he'd be okay with Kane's new plus-one. "Well, Idaho is beautiful."

He heard muffled voices as his brother communicated with Madison in the background. His brother had found the perfect assistant in Madison; hiring her was one of the best decisions he had ever made. She was neat and organized, and more importantly, she had Craig and Leah's best interests at heart. She was likely the one who suggested hiring a nanny for Idaho. Kane had noticed the longing in Craig's eyes and knew Craig saw her as more than an assistant, but his brother had never acted on his impulses.

"Madison contacted the nanny agency yesterday. We have an interview with a candidate set for tomorrow morning at ten. We've set up a conference call to join you both in the meeting room. Does that work?"

"Yeah," Kane replied.

"Perfect. There's a candidate Madison really likes, but before we make a final decision, we wanted to get your thoughts since you'll be caring for Leah with her," Craig added.

"We'll talk soon," Kane said after confirming final details. He checked his Richard Millie limited-edition watch, pleased that he still had a good chunk of the afternoon to catch up on work. Rubbing the back of his neck, he contemplated everything he had to accomplish before he left for Idaho to see his best friend.

He poured himself two fingers of scotch and headed toward the wraparound terrace, his new favorite place to relax and think. Early summer in New York was beautiful. It was a spectacular view, with rays of the afternoon sun dancing and sparkling off the Hudson River.

If he walked toward the other side of his terrace, he saw the full range of the Manhattan skyline.

KMP Towers was a forty-story building with 250 units reflecting refined urban elegance. His design focused on optimizing the light and views through spacious layouts, glass walls, and a soft palette of finishes. He had brought his vision to life, and it only deepened his desire to create more. As he leaned against the railing, swirling the amber liquid around in his glass, his thoughts drifted in time with the currents he watched.

Dread formed in the pit of his stomach as he gnawed over the details of the loan he had tried to secure to finish this very building. The bank note was a direct line to keeping his dream alive, and it evaporated. Blew up right in his face because of that damned deal he'd made with the devil, his dear old man.

He was shocked to the core when the bank called with additional loan conditions at the eleventh hour, after he had already received the pre-approval. He was a fucking Miller with plenty of money. None of the nonsense the bank had spewed made sense.

When his father offered to back the loan if Kane would agree to his nonnegotiable conditions, Kane jumped at the offer. At the time, he thought everything seemed reasonable, but the offer served as an anchor tethering him to his father's ubiquitous demands. He had unfortunately given his father leverage over him by accepting the faster solution.

His old man was cunning and brilliant, orchestrating outcomes in his favor, which made him the mogul he was today. It never occurred to Kane that his father would use those same tactics against his own son.

Three

As he got ready the next morning, Kane chose to wear a comfortable suit by the designer Ricci. As he reached for the tie lying next to his jacket, he stopped, a bit of rebellion making him smile. Just to irritate his father, he would forgo the tie today.

He did one last mental check of his place to ensure he had everything turned off or gathered for his trip before tugging his front door closed and locking it. He planned to head to the airport after his meeting with his father at PC Miller Corporation.

Kane was looking forward to seeing his best friend, Trent Jacobs. Trent had barely survived some questionable recent events as an FBI agent, which had ultimately resulted in his early retirement. In truth, the main reason for Kane's visit was to check in on him. He knew Trent was pissed off, and his pride was wounded, but at least he made the decision to start a new chapter of his life as the sheriff of Mill Creek.

After pulling up to the famed Whippler Nanny Agency, Kane slid out from the backseat of his SUV and thumped the roof with his hand. The reception area was decorated in subtle brown tones, with mahogany and marble, creating a classic yet polished look. As he entered, he glanced at the walls displaying pictures of prominent clients over the years, including his family. He and Craig had been raised by many of the nannies at this agency over the years. Kane had a growing sense of something he couldn't quite put his finger on.

Maybe his strange reaction was simply because, for the first time, he was on the hiring end of the nanny service rather than the receiving end. While he knew he needed some guidance when it came to taking care of his six-year-old niece, he was not looking forward to being around another rigid older woman who demanded absolute obedience without a hint of negotiation.

He moved to sit down in a nearby armchair when a woman entered the room from the door behind the reception desk.

"Mr. Miller, it's a pleasure to meet you. I'm Nancy, one of the managing administrators. Please follow me."

He walked behind her through a side door and down the hallway until they stopped at a conference room. She motioned him in with a wave of her arm.

"There are refreshments in the mini refrigerator," she said. "If you would like something different, just press the back office button on the phone, and we'll see if we can accommodate your request while you wait."

He nodded, took a seat, and turned his attention back to his phone. He heard the soft snick of the door as it closed. He had twenty minutes before the interview. It was plenty of time to follow up on the outstanding punch list with the head of construction at KPM Towers. Once he could close out those items, he could rent the remaining units.

After that call, he dialed up his friend and lawyer, Larry Behr. The Miller family had long used the services and resources of Behr & Goldstein, the prestigious firm owned by Larry's father, Walter. After the trouble with the last loan, he wanted to use his friend's connection with the bank to ensure there would be no last-minute surprises in securing the funding to buy that vacant lot in Manhattan for his next project. From there, once he met his father's conditions, he could initiate the quitclaim deed to KPM Towers.

He had finished wrapping up his final call when Nancy opened the door to the conference room.

"Hello again, Mr. Miller. I'd like to introduce you to Annika Bauer, the candidate your family is interviewing today."

Kane's gaze swept past Nancy as she moved aside, locking onto a stunning woman wearing a short-sleeved yellow blouse, which she'd paired with a cardigan around her shoulders. He leaned in his chair, as far to the right as he could without falling onto his face, to see if someone stood behind this person. All of his nannies growing up had either been overly maternal or had worn grim faces, as if they hadn't smiled in decades.

Annika didn't embody either of those qualities; she had to be one of the office workers. Instead, he saw a youthful woman who wore a warm smile that could melt icebergs. She had a natural beauty, with a petite build and olive skin, but more than that, she carried herself with a calm, professional air. His brother would recognize the difference and request a more mature, stoic replacement.

Then, it dawned on him. Madison, who hadn't been raised by nannies, had chosen her.

"Mr. Miller, is something wrong?" Nancy asked, her tone serious as she turned her head sideways to match his.

Fire burned his cheeks as he snapped his body upright. Annika had totally caught him off guard in the best way, and he found that idea startling. He didn't know what to say or how to rectify the scene he was causing. He gripped the back of his neck while his mind raced.

Annika's voice cut through the awkward silence. It was sweet and upbeat despite the dark smudges he now noticed under her eyes. "It's nice to meet you, Mr. Miller."

He stood, accepting her hand while his brain still raced to salvage this moment. Her hand fit perfectly inside his larger one. His body zapped at the contact of his skin on hers. He watched the women exchange brief glances before Nancy lowered her gaze to his hand, which still held Annika's.

Shit. Could he screw this meeting up anymore? He dropped her hand as if it were a hot stone and sat. Not enjoying the feeling of being examined by both women, he forced himself to relax. She deserved to be treated like a lady—someone who, he had no doubt, had the qualifications to be Leah's nanny.

"Likewise, but please call me Kane. So, you're the nanny?"

Well, that sounded horrible.

"I assure you I'm quite capable and very competent." Annika's voice washed over his heated skin.

Why was his brain short-circuiting around this woman? God, yes, of course she was competent. He was starting to appreciate her assertiveness, the sparkle in her eye, even the soft scent of lavender and vanilla that wafted with every move she made.

Craig would handle this whole misunderstanding with professionalism while Kane looked for a way to dig himself out of this hole he continued to make. Feeling more centered and controlled, he breathed a deep breath and decided that the best path forward was keeping his damn mouth shut.

Right on cue, the speaker box on the table rang, announcing an incoming call.

"I'll leave you two to your conference call. Annika, please come to see me afterward, so that we can finish your paperwork either way,"

Nancy said, shooting him a look before turning and closing the door behind her.

Annika took the seat next to him while he pressed the button to start the call.

"Good morning, Annika, Kane. We appreciate your flexibility to meet with us on such short notice," Madison said, leading the call. In the next breath, she rattled off the particulars about Leah and the expectations for this assignment.

Kane watched as Annika pulled out a folder, answering every question thoughtfully and asking several insightful ones herself. She was composed, prepared, and thoroughly competent. He inhaled slowly, waiting for his brother to state the obvious: that this incredible and skilled woman was the opposite of what they had experienced growing up. However, as the call went on, neither Craig nor Madison said anything that seemed to concern Annika.

"Annika is quite different from the nannies we had as kids. She's younger—," Kane interjected, trying to help his brother out.

"Is that an observation or a concern?" Craig interrupted.

Yes, I'm concerned. Look at her. She's perfect.

Kane turned to look at Annika, who was staring at him while she waited for his response. Her gaze followed his every movement, a brief flash of concern flickering in her beautiful brown eyes. He might have just met her, but he liked her already. Something deep inside him stirred by the mere thought that he was causing her any discomfort.

"I'm so sorry. I'm rambling. I wasn't expecting something new. I *am* impressed and know that Leah will love you," he said, hoping to negate the awkwardness of his stupid emotional reactions.

Craig jumped back into the conversation. "Precisely. This is what I want for Leah: an experience vastly different from ours, someone fun who can connect with her. Someone to laugh with her and let her be a child without squashing her dreams. I want my little girl to still believe in Santa Claus and unicorns, which is why I'm glad you can see why Annika is perfect for this job."

That made sense. His brother had insisted on raising his daughter differently, making sure he was part of her life and that she had all kinds of new experiences.

Kane saw the tiny smile that crossed Annika's face at Craig's endorsement.

A pang of regret hit him in his chest. He wanted to be the one who made her smile. He had never had such a visceral reaction to anyone before, but in one meeting, Annika had managed to impress his mind and make his body tingle. He did not know where to start untangling his feelings about her, but that would be a problem to solve...preferably before she arrived in Mill Creek with Leah.

"Kane, do you have any other questions or thoughts for Annika before we officially hire her?" Craig asked. His brother, Madison, and Annika all had their attention directed toward him.

"No, I think we've covered everything. You'll love Mill Creek. It's a special place."

Annika beamed. "I'm thrilled with this opportunity! I can't wait to meet Leah—I promise you won't regret your decision."

As he observed her genuine enthusiasm, he noticed her final comment was directed at him. He deserved to be put on notice. She was unlike most of the women he had interacted with over the years, down to earth and unafraid to speak her mind, and he found it refreshing.

Craig and Madison stayed on the line after Annika said her goodbyes and left the room. The moment she had left, Craig folded his arms across his chest as he reclined in his leather desk chair. "Care to tell me what's going on, little brother?"

"What he means is your obvious attraction to Annika," Madison interjected with a mischievous grin. When Craig snapped his head in her direction, she threw her head back with a groan. "Men can be so oblivious at times."

"Don't be dramatic. I'm just distracted and nothing more," Kane grumbled.

"If what Madison said is true, hope you can pull it together and behave yourself. She's working for us."

Kane rolled his eyes as his pulse ticked up a notch. He did not like being read like a book or that Madison had called him out. Not that her observation was wrong. "I was caught off guard, but don't worry, I can control myself around her."

Craig held Kane's gaze a moment longer. "Good, because Leah will like her. I do not want an HR situation that means Annika leaving her."

Kane swallowed his sarcastic reply, forcing a smile on his face. "Message received. I've got to run, but we'll talk later when we meet with Dad."

Kane pressed the disconnect button to end the call. This was important to Craig and Leah. He didn't need his brother's admonishment, but he agreed with his point. He did not want Annika to feel uncomfortable around him, so the next time he saw her, he would make amends. He would apologize for his behavior and show her he could act like a gentleman.

IT FELT GOOD TO have a win, Annika thought. Another step forward in getting her life back on track. As she exited the building, she raised her arm and hailed a taxi, becoming more comfortable with navigating the city. She opened the taxi door, jumped into the back seat, and gave the driver the address. Before she started her new assignment, she wanted to do a little shopping. She sat back and took in the sights as her driver pulled into the heavy traffic, a maze of small buildings surrounding her.

The interview had gone well. She really liked everyone—even Kane, surprisingly. Although she was confused by his mixed signals, his initial criticism, and ultimate support, she did not sense anything bad or deceptive about him. He seemed genuinely sincere.

She'd survived, and as much as she hated giving her stalker any power, that idea lurked, just like her bad memories. There would always be a sense of dread that she might have misread a person's intent, but she hoped that would fade over time.

On the other hand, she thought going to Mill Creek with Kane and Leah would be therapeutic. She had the agency standing behind her, and she would be staying at the sheriff's house. She closed her eyes and chanted a familiar phrase she'd formed with her therapist. *I won't let one horrible experience define my future.*

Besides, he was incarcerated.

She redirected her thoughts back to the meeting, thinking about how much one can learn about a person by observing them in action. Madison, the epitome of organization, had a sweet disposition. Craig was thoughtful yet direct in his approach; she appreciated how he gave everyone in the room an opportunity to contribute equally and be heard. Kane came across as confident but still seemed off-kilter at the meeting. She decided to chalk it up to the fact that some people have bad days.

Goodness, good genes clearly ran in the Miller family. Both brothers were handsome, but Kane reminded her of a Greek god with his chiseled face and a lean, hard body to match. His bespoke suit molded to his body like a second skin. Romance was not what this assignment was about, but a girl could dream for a moment.

She looked forward to meeting Leah. She couldn't imagine how difficult it would be for Craig to send Leah away, but she admired his protective nature, which shielded her from life's ugly truths and kept her believing in the magic of childhood.

The driver pulled to the curb near all the shops she'd spied earlier on the way to the agency. A little retail therapy was always a nice reward. She wanted to walk to each one, including the toy store across the street, to pick up a few activities to keep in her bag for Leah.

Today had been a success. The happy energy coursing through her body made her feel bold. She would walk around the area. She smiled as she remembered the fifty-dollar bill her father had given her tucked inside her footsie sock. Maybe it served as her good luck charm. *Thanks, Mom and Dad.*

At the intersection, she merged in with the multitude of people navigating down the sidewalk, pausing at the red light. When the white pedestrian image flashed on the sign, she took a deep breath and stepped forward, staying with a group of people as they all crossed the street.

See, that wasn't so bad! The smile continued to pull at her face, and she kept walking. As the crowd thinned out a little, she adjusted her speed to fall in line with another group. Feeling safe in numbers, she found the anonymity of the crowd appealing.

Her stomach rumbled, letting her know it was time for lunch. She saw a bustling sandwich joint as she approached the department store. Seeing no better advertising than a line of customers, she joined the queue and waited for her turn. After she paid, she grabbed her tray and found a spot at the counter facing the window. She opted for the special: a basil, tomato, and mozzarella cheese sandwich, drizzled with balsamic glaze. She loved the flavors and the smell of the freshly baked bread.

A while later, she checked the time and laughed. She had so much fun that she completely lost track of time while she shopped her way through makeup, clothing, shoes, and lingerie. For her final stop, she needed to head to the toy store. She exited the enormous building, taking a moment to orient herself when she noticed she had to backtrack to her next destination.

Not many people were out on the street at this time of day. A businessman passed her, his phone to his ear, as he walked in the direction she needed to go. She approached the signal when the man she followed had decided to dart across the street. Instead, she stopped dead in her tracks and waited for the message to indicate she could cross. But the problem was that no one stood with her, and no one was approaching her.

Nervous energy crawled up her spine. She gripped the handles of her shopping bags harder while her heart hammered in her chest. She gulped down a deep breath. When the light flashed to walk, she couldn't move her feet as if they had become one with the sidewalk. The signal flashed and turned red, so she decided to wait for the next one. Another glance over her shoulder, and still, no one approached.

Hello, NYC, where is everyone? Her hands started to shake, her breathing became labored, and her skin prickled as she realized that she had to cross the street alone. People walk across busy streets every day in America.

When the light changed for the second time, she saw a bicycle fly past on her right into the traffic in her peripheral vision. The piercing hi-lo siren from an approaching emergency vehicle sounded. A car screeched its brakes as the bicyclist swerved to miss the car. More horns blared. Annika's head began to spin, and her vision blackened toward the edges. She staggered backward a few steps, collapsing on the ground. She rubbed her hand over the ugly scar on her right leg, closing her eyes and forcing herself to take several deep breaths.

The last thing she wanted to do was barf on the sidewalk after falling unceremoniously to the cement.

"Ma'am, you okay? Are you hurt?" A man dressed in a business suit asked as he squatted next to her.

Where had he been two minutes ago? And how do you answer that question without anger and fear lacing each word? She knew she was not being fair, but she was beyond frustrated that her adventurous afternoon had crashed and burned. *Damn, my stalker! Damn him to hell!*

"I'm fine. I lost my balance with all the commotion," she replied in a shaky voice. "Thanks for being so kind."

Annika accepted the man's hand and stood up, making sure she had all her bags. She forced herself to smile at him, then propelled her feet to move her forward. She hailed a cab as quickly as she could and escaped.

Four

KANE ARRIVED AT HIS father's building in Lower Manhattan ahead of schedule. He had learned at a young age that tardiness meant being rescheduled. To his father, it did not matter the reason; if you were late, you were not valuing his time.

He had always loved PC Miller Corporation's building. Listed by the Landmarks Preservation Commission, it was a twenty-five-floor architectural gem with its neo-Renaissance style and unobstructed views of the harbor and nearby park. The marble floor of the lobby gleamed as he strode toward the bank of elevators.

As the small elevator car climbed to the top floor, he mentally reviewed his talking points for the Alaska project he'd been tasked with completing. The ding signaled his arrival before the doors slid open to reveal his father's executive assistant waiting for him. Although young and very attractive, unspoken prerequisites for his father, she was also uncompromisingly loyal to Bruce Miller. His father was not an easy man to please and demanded more of those in his employ than he gave. Kane could not figure out why she enjoyed working for him.

"Good morning, Mr. Miller," she greeted him with a broad smile. "Mr. Miller is ready for you. Do you need anything, sir?"

"No, I'm good," he replied.

She'd moved ahead of him to open the large wooden door to his father's office. Decorated in blue and brown hues, with natural light coming in from the floor-to-ceiling windows, the room felt inviting and calm. The walls are adorned with various framed articles and memorabilia showcasing PC Miller's history, contributions, and successes. Surprisingly, even a family portrait hung on the wall, taken when he was eight and his brother was twelve. A sitting area with two small couches and a coffee table between them took up the middle of the room. One corner of the office featured a small, round conference table, while the other corner housed a wet bar and a private bathroom.

"Were you worth my time and investment in KPM Towers while you were in Alaska?" Bruce inquired, not lifting his head from the report he was flipping through at his large wooden desk. "We want to win points for optics."

"I did my part. I designed the library, community center, and elementary school to be modern in form and function. Each facility has cutting-edge technology, including solar capabilities for the summer months." Kane moved toward his father, taking a seat in one of the two chairs facing his desk. He dropped a folder on the desk that held pictures of all the structures, along with the dedication celebration. "Take a look for yourself."

He waited for his father to gather the pages of his report before picking up the folder. "As for the optics, your presence would have been welcome," he added.

When his father had relented and allowed him to attend the university of his choosing to major in architecture, it had meant so much to Kane. He had thought his father had finally accepted that he had zero interest in corporate life, that mining would never be a part of his present or future. He appreciated what his family had built, but working for the family business would have drained the life from him.

Luckily, Craig loved all aspects of mining and could not wait to take over the empire someday. His brother had so many ideas on how to evolve and strengthen the company for generations to come. When Craig became the next Chief Operating Officer, he would make an amazing leader, one who was the opposite of his father in many ways.

"You were in charge of the design and construction of each structure, not equipping them with books, computers, and the like. You exceeded the budget without approval. Son, I expect adherence in all matters." Bruce tossed the folder to the side. His stern voice interrupted Kane's thoughts.

Kane barely suppressed the rise of his pulse. Nothing good would come from arguing with him. He would never admit that his father's reluctance to admire his architectural achievements hurt.

His father was a well-honed replica of his grandfather, lacking the intrinsic qualities of being a loving, nurturing human being. There were moments when his father surprised him, like when he let him attend Cornell to earn his degree, and he had started to wonder if deep down his father harbored bereft feelings from his childhood. However, in the end, his father was still who he chose to be. Kane sat in his father's office today to figure out a way out of the whole predicament of his father's disingenuous loan offer. That knowledge pissed him off the most.

"I got approval from Craig when you refused to answer my phone calls," Kane retorted. "As for optics, I exceeded expectations. The community loves the PC Miller Corporation as much as they love my buildings. A complete win-win."

Before his father could say anything, Kane added, "I'm working on the Miller Library project in Montana next, leaving me only one more condition to satisfy."

His father sent him a warning, steepling his fingers together in front of his face as he rested his elbows on his desk. "I was too lenient with you growing up. You report directly to me, not your brother. I will decide when each condition has been met. I want the plans for Montana next week."

So much for taking the high road. Kane felt compelled to share a few observations of his own, since his father had decided to head down that path.

"Lenient isn't a word you earned; that would imply you participated in or cared about my childhood. It's a shame you and Mom missed so much of my life, unless you both consider being absentee parents is an accomplishment."

Kane watched his father's nostrils flare before he stood and walked around his large desk. Bruce perched himself on the edge of the desk, staring down at him. His father likely got away with more than he should because he was handsome even as he got older. He looked distinguished with subtle wrinkles and grayish-black eyebrows set against a chiseled face framed by thick white hair.

"Son, emotions have no place in business. Difficult choices must be made, and some require personal sacrifice. Through generations of Millers, this company was built on that expectation. Less emotion leads to better decision-making, greater loyalty, and the right outcome every time. Thank God, we have Craig; he understands this. He is excelling under my tutelage."

Kane sat quietly, holding his father's glare.

His father pointed his finger at him. "Now, it's time for you to step up and do your part in upholding the Miller name."

It appeared the devil was in a mood today. After several seconds of silence, his father continued. "As my last condition, you are to marry the daughter of Thomas Monroe, the Secretary of the Interior, no later than next month. This union with Samantha Monroe is crucial for this family and for the PC Miller Corporation."

"You've lost your damned mind." Kane's voice was heavy with disdain. "I would have thought you would've learned your lesson after what happened when you tried to enforce this stupid Miller legacy nonsense on Craig."

If his father's stare could have shot daggers, Kane would have been bleeding. "You're not naïve enough to think we were just born lucky. This marriage, whether you like it or not, is the priority."

Kane lowered his head, allowing a few seconds to pass before he responded. "You're delusional. Maybe this company needs new leadership."

Bruce whirled, slamming his palm down on his desk with a loud boom. "Enough! I don't appreciate your disobedience. You have no idea what it takes to run a global conglomerate. You have no idea what is at stake."

"What's at stake?" Kane glowered at his father. "It must be pretty important if you're willing to tether my life to it."

"Your union is critical to allowing PCM to gain insight into the inner workings of our government and influence policy. How do you think anything gets done in this country?" Bruce composed himself. "There isn't a moment to waste. At seven o'clock tonight, my driver will bring Samantha to your place to meet you."

Kane rubbed his hand across his neck. "What has she been told, exactly?"

"I don't know the specifics. The important part is that her father and I are aligned. Since she has signed a nondisclosure agreement, she knows everything you two discuss is privileged information. My lawyers are still working on the prenup and the marriage contract. Once you and Ms. Monroe sign the paperwork, your engagement will be announced."

Kane sat as his world tilted off its axis. He had not thought he would be subjected to that part of the Miller marriage tradition, especially after the blowup of Craig's marriage.

"It's time to conference in your brother." His father was business as usual as he started pressing a series of buttons. Bruce did not display an ounce of remorse as he took control of the call, moving through a list of questions and updates from a notepad in his hand.

When it was his brother's turn to speak, Craig laid out the situation in London. "Warwick Mine is close to re-opening, but could be compromised with the uproar this has caused within the community. With the media and Global Peace and Harmony on-site, Legal and Corporate Relations have their hands full trying to control the narrative and head off the spread of misinformation. The riots and protests are getting out of hand. I don't want Leah caught in the middle of it. I'm—"

Bruce interrupted abruptly. "There will always be problems in this world; running from hardships doesn't make them disappear. This mine will reopen on time. I want the onboarding of senior leadership completed before you move back to New York."

"My daughter will always come first. I'm simply informing you of the situation and that I'll be sending my daughter home early." Craig's immediate yet forceful reply impressed Kane. "I have no plans to leave until Steven Ashcroft's transition into the role of Executive Vice President of European Operations is complete."

"Good. I won't tolerate delays, Craig," Bruce said.

"I'm aware of your priorities, but now you understand mine. That is not a lesson I'll be teaching Leah anytime soon."

Kane admired his brother for many reasons, his fierce loyalty to and protection over his daughter among them. He made one hell of a good father, especially as the opposite of their own. Craig would always protect the best interests of PC Miller Corporation, but family, friends, and employees came first.

Kane cleared his throat. “Leah will be safe with me, although I’m sure she will also be counting down the days until you come home. She's a daddy's girl.”

“I’ll miss her terribly, but she’s thrilled about visiting Idaho with her favorite uncle,” Craig said, voice steady over the sound of him shuffling paperwork in the background.

Their father’s eyes narrowed. “You’re going to Idaho? You know you have time-sensitive business to attend to.”

Kane nodded. “How could I ever forget? You remind me at every opportunity.”

When he was younger, Kane had a bully who was making his life a living hell. One day, he was summoned to his father’s office, where his father gave him advice on how to handle his unpleasant situation. *You were right to use your brain over your fists. The part you missed was finding his weakness and exploiting it. Never underestimate the power of vulnerability; it can help you neutralize your enemy.*

Kane’s stomach tightened as he recognized that his father was using the same tactic on him. He needed to get out of here. He cut into the conversation. “I know you two have more business to conduct, so I'm going to head out.”

“Thanks again, little brother,” Craig’s voice boomed over the speaker.

As Kane exited the office, he thought about his parents’ marriage. They had also been arranged to further business relations. While he knew his parents were not madly in love, they had developed a partnership. Beyond that, he was not sure whether they shared the same hobbies or interests. Hell, he did not even know whether they shared the same bed.

To retain his one true love, being an architect and running his own design firm, Kane would have to follow in the idiotic tradition, too. His father's deal reminded him that his father was not helping him, but rather controlling him. He was a damn fool for accepting. His father might have won that round, but Kane was not going to let him keep winning. His focus was on paying his father back quickly so he could put distance between them.

He sent Trent a text to let him know he had to wrap up a few things and would fly out the next morning instead. When he got a thumbs-up reply from him, he let out a deep breath.

STEPPING OUT ONTO HIS deck, Kane moved toward the railing, watching the current undulate on the Hudson as boats returned to the docks for the night. His head pounded from his long day of meetings. It didn't please him that he had to push back his departure for Idaho. He had thought about postponing this meeting until he returned, but he didn't have the patience to deal with his father's tirade. According to his watch, Samantha would be arriving in a few minutes. What an awkward meeting this would be, and how do you even start the conversation? *Hi, wife-to-be, how does it feel to be stuck with me? God help us, this sucks.*

The normally pleasant chime of the doorbell hit him square in the stomach like a one-two punch. He took the last sip of his whiskey, desperately trying to figure out where to start this conversation. Coming up empty, his frustration soared. When he opened the front door, he was not expecting a beautiful woman in a black strapless cocktail dress paired with red stilettos. She was a bombshell with almond-shaped blue eyes and big, pouty lips painted in red lipstick that matched her shoes. Any man would look better when she adorned his side. The problem he had with this scenario? He didn't want an accessory.

"Hello, Samantha, I'm Kane. Please come inside," he said, pushing the door wider to allow her to enter. While she was composed and had dressed for the occasion, her face held zero happiness, and her body remained ramrod straight. She gazed at him cautiously, probably assessing him and deciding her fate. Finally, a wisp of a smile crossed her lips right before she passed by him, the soft scent of her perfume lingering in the air.

"Hi, which way do I go?" She held out a slender hand in greeting. "You'll have to forgive me, I'm not sure what's expected of me in this situation. I've never had a relationship mapped out in legal papers. I'm sure you're a pro, so I'll look to you for guidance."

He motioned for her to follow him to the living room. He hadn't expected such bold honesty, but it felt like a hopeful place to start. "Unfortunately, it's the blind leading the blind. I'm not any more familiar with navigating any of that than you. In fact, I just learned about you this afternoon."

As she sat down in the chair, her eyebrows scrunched together. "Are you serious?"

He nodded, taking a seat on the couch. "What were you told?"

"Just that you'll be my husband and I'll be your perfect wife and mother to our children. That this union would benefit all parties involved, whatever the hell that means." She paused before composing herself. "At this point, I've only signed the NDA. I was put on notice while the contracts are still being finalized to get on board with my exciting future and disassociate myself with everyone from my past."

Kane bristled when he heard that a baby clause was coming. He had zero desire to have children. He knew Craig's marriage was to produce an heir, but his marriage ended when Penelope left with her two-million-dollar settlement after Leah was born. He would bet his building that his father closed that loophole and made any future agreements ironclad.

While he didn't know much about her, she'd sounded sad as she spoke of cutting off the people she knew and loved in her life. "I have no real right to ask, so forgive me for asking this question, but are you just talking about your friends, or is there a boyfriend in the middle of this?"

Her head snapped up, her gaze flashing before she got herself under control. "I...uh...have a boyfriend. We've been together for six years."

"I'm sorry, Samantha, I can't imagine what you're going through right now." His stomach churned with dread. This stupid arrangement was costing her far more than it was him. Where he could request a mistress clause, allowing him to sleep with whomever he wanted as long as the other conditions were met, but Samantha's contract would offer no such relief. His *perfect* wife would be bound to be him, and him only, forever.

After a moment of tense silence, Kane asked, "Do you even want to have children?"

"I did, once *my* boyfriend and I married. I don't want them with you, or anyone my father deems fit to sell my body to." She scoffed. "It doesn't matter if it's for *the greater good.*"

Kane sank his head back into the sofa. This was so fucked up. The only commonality they shared at that point was that they were children of men who would use them for their own personal gain. He had no doubt that her father wanted access to the Miller wealth and connections, while his father wanted the power that Monroe's political position offered.

Samantha broke into his ruminating thoughts. "You are the lucky man who gets me, but you are even luckier because I'm an amazing person. I refuse to be bitter and resentful toward you for the rest of my life, so we need to make the best of this situation."

He blew out an irritated breath and lifted his head. "I need a scotch. How about you?"

She nodded eagerly. He walked to the bar, reached for his prized bottle of Macallan, and poured two fingers into two crystal glasses before turning to hand her one. "Let's go out on the deck. I think we could both use some fresh air."

Once outside, he smiled as she gasped. It *was* a spectacular view. He watched her walk to the railing, slowly taking in the sights.

He did not want a marriage like the one his parents had. Rather, he desired what Albert and Linda shared, a relationship based on love and adoration. If he ever chose to get married, he wanted a wife, a best friend, who shared his interests and had intense chemistry with him.

Annika's smiling face popped into his head, lightening the emptiness he was feeling. There was something so refreshingly different about her that just made him smile when he thought of her. Nothing about her seemed calculated. What you saw was what you would get. She was not afraid to express her emotions while sharing her opinions. When he held her hand at the interview, he knew he never wanted to break that connection between them.

"Is he the one you can't see yourself living without?" he asked thoughtfully.

Samantha turned toward him, radiating happiness at the thought of her boyfriend. Before she even spoke, he already knew the answer. "Yes."

"Keep this between us for now, but don't stop seeing him. We'll figure out how to reverse this proposal one way or another."

Samantha sat up straighter, suspicion narrowing her eyes. "I don't mean any disrespect, but how do I know you actually mean that? That you aren't going to run to your father about him?"

This is why he hated manipulation.

"Because I'm the one orchestrating this rebellion against my father." He paused, holding her gaze for a few seconds while she processed his words. "I guess we'll have to trust each other if we want to change this outcome."

She reached out her hand. "Please make this stop, Kane, and you have a deal."

Kane accepted her handshake. "I'm leaving tomorrow for Idaho to visit a friend, but let me give you my number. If you need me for any reason, call me."

After he added her number to his contacts, he offered her one extra piece of reassurance, shooting her a short text for her to keep. *Don't stop seeing your boyfriend. I'll speak with my father about ending this betrothal.*

Her phone dinged, and she pulled it out to read the message.

Her mouth dropped open. "Thank you. For what it's worth, you are not anything like I thought you'd be."

"I promise we'll find a solution." He was glad his words brought her a measure of comfort.

She smiled softly in return.

He liked her smile; however, it did not have the same effect as Annika's.

After escorting her down the elevator to the lobby, he stayed downstairs until she was safely in the hired car, then headed back to wherever she was staying in the city.

He and Samantha had a plan and shared common ground. He could keep Samantha tied to the man she loved, and he would stay on track with his architectural business.

The night had turned out to be better than he expected.

Five

Kane woke up just as the captain was announcing that they were preparing to land. Thursday morning had come much too early after a fitful night of sleep, and he was thankful for the extra hours of sleep he got in the comfy leather recliner chair as the plane flew to Mill Creek, Idaho.

While this trip had a purpose, the timing of it could not have been better. He needed a reprieve from his father's machinations. Instead, he was looking forward to spending some quality time with Leah.

The aircraft door opened, letting sunlight filter into the cabin, illuminating tiny dust particles in its rays. Kane gathered his bags and headed toward the exit, thanking the crew as he descended the portable stairs. As his feet hit the tarmac, his head swiveled in search of his best friend. He nearly missed Trent, standing just outside the glass doors of the private terminal with his back against that opposite wall. You can take the man out of the FBI, but you can't take the FBI out of the man. Kane chuckled to himself.

As he approached, Trent met him halfway until both men could extend their hands to each other, which turned into a back-slapping hug.

"It's been way too long," Kane said, leaning toward his friend to be heard over the cacophony of airport noises surrounding them.

"I see you dressed properly for the mountains in your fashionable and uncomfortable-looking suit."

Kane slapped his friend's back. "I think you're a closet fashionista, since you always comment on my clothing."

"Sure, keep telling yourself that lie." Trent barked out his laughter. "When I left the FBI, the suits went with it. I'm parked over here."

Kane followed Trent through the private terminal and outside to the small parking area, where Trent's sheriff's vehicle waited. "Sweet! Do we get to use the siren? You can check off a fantasy from my youth."

Trent fixed him with a look. "My siren isn't a toy. It's for official business only, and I'm here in a personal capacity."

Kane shrugged. "Sirens are cool. All I get is a drafting table and a hard hat."

"Maybe you chose the wrong career," Trent grumbled, pulling out his key fob to unlock the doors. "I'm on vacation with no plans to use it."

The new vehicle smell hit Kane as soon as he opened the door to the Ford F250 Super Duty.

"I like your new ride. I couldn't imagine driving this monster around the city. I prefer smaller and faster vehicles."

Trent shot his friend a look. "News flash: driving in New York City is torture."

They both burst out laughing. As Trent drove toward the mountains, Kane's body swayed with the pull and lean of each turn as the road snaked upward. He listened as his friend spoke like a tour guide, pointing out landscape features and providing updates on the surrounding area.

It was nothing but magnificent views, the bluest sky framed by the whitest, puffy clouds he'd ever seen. Pine trees lined the hillsides while clusters of aspen swayed in the wind. He could almost hear the leaves' melodic quiver. The scene was completed by the creek that ran alongside the road. He loved the beauty of wide open space.

"One of my greatest memories is when we visited your grandpa during the summer of our sophomore year in college," Kane said over the hum of the engine.

Trent checked his mirrors before passing a truck pulling an RV. "Mine too, although I remember you not being a great camper. Your little misadventure will always make me laugh."

Kane did not realize how much he missed their easy banter. Trent might not be blood, but he was still his brother.

He was relieved to see his friend doing better, at least outwardly, since his retirement from the FBI. The last few months had been hard on Trent, with his injuries, the death of his partner, and the mess that followed, leading to his retirement. When his grandfather passed shortly thereafter, Kane worried that his friend might just dig himself a hole and give up, although to his surprise, Trent did end up running to fill his grandfather's open seat at the sheriff's department.

Trent still did not talk much about any of it, but Kane knew grieving and dealing with trauma took time. Through all of it, Kane tried to make sure Trent knew he was in his corner.

"That story will be kept strictly between us. I'm a rich man who has serious legal counsel at my disposal. I'm not opposed to using it to protect my innocence," Kane replied, giving him a smirk.

"It's not your innocence you're protecting. It's your man card," Trent countered.

Kane couldn't help but laugh. In his defense, at the time, he had never spent the night outside in the dense forest where there were lots of strange noises and wild animals. That night, he had really thought a bear was lurking in their camp, ready to eat them. To this day, his idea of camping was more along the lines of staying at a lodge or five-star hotel that happened to be surrounded by forest.

"If you really want to make this a competition, let's see how you handle yourself using a bidet or which piece of cutlery to use in a twelve-plus place setting during a formal dinner while engaging in socially acceptable small talk in a tuxedo."

"Dude, you win. I would rather curl up in the fetal position," Trent groaned.

Trent pulled off the highway towards the city of Mill Creek. It was small but quaint. Kane appreciated the warmth and friendliness on full display as they drove through town. People waved at Trent as he passed by, making it clear that he was more than the sheriff in this township. In New York, people kept to themselves or to the group they walked with. If you drove, you focused on the organized chaos of the traffic.

"Unless their itinerary has changed, Madison and Leah should be arriving in New York this afternoon. Annika will meet them at the airport before the three of them fly here on Friday," Kane said.

"I can't wait to meet Leah," Trent said as he turned onto Main Street. "Someday, we need to get Craig to visit."

Kane nodded as he palmed his phone to see if he had any updates from his brother or Madison.

Trent turned on his blinker. "So, what's Annika like?"

Kane paused, trying to think about how to describe the woman who had occupied his mind since meeting her. He kept telling himself that it was because he had made an ass of himself, but there was something about her that stuck with him.

"Quite the opposite from the multitude of nannies we had growing up. She's great—young, warm... beautiful. She's perfect for Leah."

"Is she single or—"

Kane saw red, turning his head sharply toward his friend. "She's here to take care of Leah. That's it, and nothing more."

Trent shot his friend a sideways glance, a smirk covering his face. "Duly noted."

Kane peered out the window. *Great*, he had overreacted by misjudging his friend's inquiry.

He took in his surroundings to clear his mind. Mill Creek was a mix of old charm and modern updates, with wooden storefronts and plank-board sidewalks connecting each store to newer buildings with bright-colored siding. He imagined the city park, the town's perfect centerpiece, bustling with activity on weekends.

As if reading his mind, Trent pointed down the road facing the park. "This Saturday is a movie-in-the-park night. The whole town attends with blankets, lawn chairs, and picnic baskets. It's all the rage. We should take Leah."

What a great use of the space to bring the community together. Kane leaned into the idea. His father wanted to rewrite the narrative of PC Miller, showing the company enriched towns and communities. Perhaps Kane could incorporate something similar into the Miller Library project. He could create a large grassy area in front of the building for the community to enjoy for movies, picnics, reading, and more.

"What's playing?"

"Hmm, I'm not sure, but it will be a family movie. Irene, our resident librarian, coordinates with the community center."

"I think Leah would love to go. Be careful, though. Leah's a social butterfly. I guarantee she'll know more people than you by the end of the night. My mother is always admonishing Craig, telling him his daughter lacks dignity and discipline, that she's too much of a free spirit."

"She's six, right? Aren't children supposed to explore and discover shit?"

Kane laughed. "Exactly, and that's why she's spending time with me instead of the grandparents."

"You know, it's amazing that you and your brother turned out the way you did, considering you were raised by societal robots who sucked at being loving parents." Trent slapped Kane's shoulder as he pulled into his driveway.

"I can always count on you for keeping it real, Dr. Phil." Kane flashed Trent a wry smile.

He popped open the passenger door, a smile crossing his face as memories of time spent here came back. Looking forward to relaxing, he followed Trent inside with his luggage.

After spending the afternoon shooting the shit and goofing around, they barbecued steaks and baked potatoes for dinner. They sat on the deck enjoying the setting sun, listening to the creek babble in the distance over stones and debris. Nestled back from the main road, tucked behind pine trees and shrubbery, the cabin offered a beautiful landscape and privacy. Along one side of the property, a smaller creek flowed into the bigger one at the bottom of the hill, lined by clusters of aspen trees. Even the bugs added their distinct sounds to the melody of the natural surroundings.

Kane had always enjoyed spending time here. When he was younger, he could not imagine living here full-time, but now he has realized he no longer shares that opinion. He could easily imagine himself enjoying the best of both worlds: a house in the city and another in the mountains.

"Why's that goofy look on your face?" Trent asked, handing him an empty plate.

"Just admiring the view. It's beautiful. I might just move here at some point."

Trent's eyes widened. "Don't tease me, just do it. I wouldn't mind having you closer. Now, get your city-slicker, over-dressed ass into the kitchen to load your potato while I bring the steaks inside."

Deciding to eat on the porch, they both brought their plates back outside. For several minutes, the only sound was the scraping of metal on ceramic. Kane had eaten in some of the finest steak houses in the world, but Trent's barbecuing skills were legendary. When he finished his meal, he took his plate to the sink, adding it to the stack sitting in it, and grabbed two more beers from the kitchen.

"Grab the light?" Trent hollered from the chair before he returned with the beer.

The moment Kane flipped the switch, the deck plunged into darkness. As his eyes adjusted, he swept his gaze up toward the sky, gasping. A million stars, brilliant white lights, twinkled back at him, illuminating the sky. It was a sight you could never enjoy in the city with all the artificial lights.

Kane took his seat. "Now that you own this piece of paradise, are you planning to modernize it?" The cabin had belonged to Trent's grandfather, who left it to him upon his passing. He was glad his friend chose to stay here, but he could do with a creature comfort or two.

"I don't know." Trent propped his feet up on the railing. "I haven't had the time since being elected Sheriff. My staff has forgotten that protecting Mill Creek's citizens and resources should be a priority, even on most days when it was painfully quiet. It's hard to drill the concept that preparedness is critical to success, so all my time goes to developing and training my deputies."

"I bet that your team is seeing the bigger picture now that you're here."

"It's certainly shown me who is struggling to perform or evolve. I think they understand my expectations, but it's a work in progress, that's for sure."

"What about renovating?" Kane pressed his finger into Trent's arm. "Don't think I fell for your subtle re-direct of my original question."

Trent took a swig from his bottle. "Honestly, I've been dragging my feet. I like living in *his* house. If I do anything to it, I may not recognize this place as my grandfather's."

"Your grandfather wanted you to have this house. No amount of improvement or maintenance will alter your memories or his presence. It's like you're carrying on his legacy by building your own on top of his foundation."

Trent took another swig of his beer before responding. "Who are you? When did you become so balanced and logical?"

"You've got to live your life, man. Quit beating yourself up over things you can't control."

"Moving forward is harder than it sounds...your mind still has access to the past and drags it along," Trent answered flatly.

Kane sensed his friend was talking about his last assignment in the FBI. He hated seeing him struggle with everything that had happened, but they sat in companionable silence while his friend worked through his thoughts.

"Hypothetically, if I wanted to take on that challenge, I would need to hire an architect. One that I trust," Trent said, breaking the silence. "Someone who understands the importance of this home and would find the right balance of preservation and renovation."

Kane smiled. "I might know a guy. He's expensive but dresses impeccably."

Their laughter filled the night mountain air.

"So," Kane turned toward his friend, curious if he would share whatever he had been thinking about. "How are you doing with everything, Trent?"

Trent was silent for a long moment. "Guilt is a bitch, and she's got her grip on me. It's all a process, but in the end, I still let down the people I care most about."

Kane leaned his head back against the wall, letting out a measured breath. "I worry about you. You had so much shit hit you all at once—"

"Look, Kane." Trent sighed. "I appreciate you checking in, but I don't want to discuss any of it. Let's just enjoy our time together."

Kane sat still, letting his friend's words fade until only the surrounding sounds of the mountain remained. It took every bit of restraint not to push, but he respected his friend's request. "I'm here for you today, tomorrow, or in the future. All you have to do is say the word."

Trent rolled his head toward him. "I know, Kane."

Kane's phone chirped with an incoming text from Madison. "Leah and Madison are in New York and heading our way tomorrow with Annika."

Trent nodded, then put his beer on the table between their chairs and dropped his legs from the railing. "I'm almost afraid to ask, but how's Bruce? Did he like the work you did in Alaska?"

Trent couldn't help himself. Kane laughed and filled him in on how the meeting went the other day, including how his father dismissed Craig for wanting to send Leah home early to avoid the rioting protestors in London. Aside from Craig and Larry, Trent was Kane's closest confidant. When he needed a direct answer, he knew he could always turn to his friend.

"My father announced I'm now required to marry as the last condition for his bailout financing," Kane said. "I pushed my flight yesterday to meet the woman he picked for me, Samantha Monroe. She's the daughter of the Secretary of the Interior."

Trent rubbed his hand over his face. "I thought that whole idiotic Miller family tradition was finished after Penelope broke the agreement by leaving your brother and Leah behind. I don't want to speak ill of the dead, but she left a mess for Craig to explain to Leah when she's older."

Craig really tried to make Penelope happy while they were together, even going toe-to-toe with their father to grant her the divorce she wanted. Then, after she died in a car accident, Craig had shut down. He still had not fully recovered from the disaster of his marriage or its aftermath.

"I did too, but I can only imagine the changes he made to the contract and payout schedules after that fiasco." Kane sipped on his beer, hoping to wash down the bitterness of the arrangement.

"I don't mean to be sappy, but if I ever get married, I want love, lust, and everything in between. Have you told Craig?" Trent asked.

Kane knew Trent didn't understand his family's expectations, the politics behind everything they did. Arranged marriages, as barbaric as they seemed, were part of a strategic union that was more common than anyone knew. But he didn't want what happened to Penelope and Craig to happen to him.

"No, he's got enough on his plate now. I'm hoping to end this before there's anything to say," he replied. "Samantha, however, doesn't want this any more than I do. She has a boyfriend she is in love with and wants to keep. So, we're figuring it out while I try to reason with my father."

"I don't mean to spoil your grand plan, but Bruce isn't really into compromises. Reasoning with him seems like a long shot," Trent said.

"An iron-clad contract only matters if the signer cares about the conditions. I know you don't understand my family's inner dynamics. I'm not defending it, but these are the facts. Just remember this knowledge isn't public," Kane said.

Trent ran his hand through his hair and exhaled. "I'll always tell you my views just like I'll always have your back, Kane. But my lips are sealed."

ANNIKA COULD NOT STOP grinning from ear to ear as she sat in the plush leather recliner on the Miller private jet. She had never experienced any kind of luxury like this; she felt like a movie star.

Great, now I'm ruined for life.

She took her e-reader from her bag and continued reading her romance novel. She hoped someday she would find a man who would accept her entirely and love her unconditionally, like the hero in her book.

This assignment was progress toward her recovery. The agency did put a safety protocol in place for her. They would check in and, if she felt overwhelmed or needed to terminate early, she just had to use a pre-established code phrase. She still felt a small riot of nerves in her stomach thinking about the unknown, but she also knew not every new situation would lead to the same paralyzing trauma she had survived. Determined to move forward, she would embrace this adventure and focus on leaving those fears in the past.

Not feeling like reading, she twisted her chair to find Madison, who had been on the phone since they left New York. She was very pretty, with a curvy figure, long brown hair that fell to her shoulders, and matching eyes. Madison's hands moved animatedly as she spoke or whenever she picked up a pen to jot down a note.

"Finally! I'm so sorry to be rude. You step out of the office and poof, everything goes haywire," Madison said a few minutes later, as she sank down in a nearby recliner. "How are you doing, Annika?"

"I'm great. This is a mighty fine way to travel. How are *you* feeling?"

"Aside from being awake too long, I'm good. I'm looking forward to a long, hot bath and a solid ten hours of sleep in my own bed."

The flight attendant appeared from the back of the plane. "Ma'am, we have forty-five minutes before we begin our descent into the Boise airport. Can I get you anything before we land?"

Madison smiled up at the woman. "I'd love a Coke and half of a chicken salad sandwich. Annika, anything for you?"

"No, thank you. I ate earlier," Annika responded to the attendant.

She liked Madison. She appreciated the familiarity and ease they had established in a short time, starting with the very first phone call. When Annika went back to the toy store, it was easy to call Madison for some insight on a few surprises to bring along for Leah while they were in Mill Creek. If distance were not an issue, she could see them becoming friends.

The attendant returned with her plate and drink, leaving it on the surface Madison had just cleared.

"Do you head back to New York today, or are you staying here for a few days?" Annika asked

Madison dabbed the corner of her mouth with a linen napkin. "Unfortunately, I do have to head back. There are quite a few things I need to accomplish in New York before I return to London. Craig is lost without my assistance for too long. That man is brilliant, don't get me wrong, but he needs someone to help organize the bazillion balls he juggles every day."

Annika laughed. "Behind every successful man stands a woman."

"Exactly." Madison smiled, raising her glass towards Annika.

"Will moving back to the States be a good thing?"

"Absolutely. Craig's workload will slow down, which is a bonus. His father can be quite demanding, and Craig has gone nonstop since moving to London to establish the European Headquarters," Madison said, taking the last bite of her sandwich. "But, I'll miss the majestic beauty of London."

"Does Leah ever spend time with her mother?" Annika asked curiously. When Madison's face hardened and pushed her plate to the side, she felt like her question might have crossed a line. "Never mind—I didn't mean to overstep. I only wanted to be prepared in case Leah mentioned her."

"Please don't apologize. It's an innocent question." Madison paused before continuing. "Nothing about Penelope, Leah's mother, is easy to answer. I don't know much about her, other than she walked away from Leah and Craig, demanding a divorce and causing a great deal of pain in the process. She unfortunately was killed in a horrific car accident two years after the divorce, but Leah knows her mom is in heaven."

Annika got the gist; she was fascinated by what seemed like a real-life soap opera, but she needed to remember that behind each juicy tidbit of information, there was a person whose feelings had been hurt. "Understood. If Leah brings anything up, I'll listen but direct her to speak to her father."

Madison nodded, moving the stack of papers she had earlier into her briefcase. "Craig's a wonderful father and a man who puts his daughter first. Speaking of Princess Leah, it can take a bit of time for her to wake up if she's overly tired. Let me go get her up and moving."

After a few minutes, Madison returned, taking her seat on the sofa and fastening her seatbelt. "She's ready to go, but must have an apple juice before we land."

Right on cue, Leah bounded from the back of the plane toward the galley, running up to Madison and thrusting herself into her arms.

If Annika did not know the story, she would have assumed that Madison was Leah's mother. She watched Madison lean down and whisper into her ear. A second later, Leah jumped off her lap, turning towards Annika with her little hand extended.

"I'm Leah."

Annika accepted her hand. "I'm Annika. It's so nice to meet you."

"You're pretty, like Madison," Leah said before returning to sit down next to Madison.

"Well, thank you, Leah," Annika replied. "You are too."

Leah slurped down the last of her juice box before heading back to the galley to throw away her empty container. When Leah returned, she announced, "We gonna land."

Madison gently corrected her wording and waited for Leah to update her announcement.

"We are going to land."

"Good girl, Leah."

Once the plane's wheels touched down on the tarmac and the flight door opened, Madison handed Annika a folded piece of thick paper. "I'm glad we found you. You'll be good for Leah and Kane."

Annika smiled at her kind words, quickly reading the note as she ushered Leah toward the front of the plane.

Here's my phone number—call anytime. I consider us friends.

Annika's smile widened as she refolded the paper, tucking it into her purse. Taking a deep breath, she squared her shoulders, gathered her bags, and headed toward the exit and down the staircase.

Hello, world. I'm back!

Six

"UNCLE KANE! UNCLE KANE!" Leah squealed as she raced down the steps of the plane.

Kane bent down to scoop Leah up into his arms, giving her a bear hug. "I can't believe how big you've gotten! I've missed you."

Leah shrieked and squeezed him back. "I missed you, too."

She pushed back a little so she could frame his face with her tiny hands. "Don't be sad, Uncle Kane. We're here to take care of you," Leah said before she explained how she and Annika were going to take care of him and Trent.

Kane's face froze in surprise and a touch of confusion at her comment.

Madison laughed as she approached, sliding right into his outstretched arm for a hug. "Craig told Leah that you and Trent need care, so he sent his daughter to help out."

He put his niece down and grabbed her hand. "Leah, Madison, please meet my best friend, Trent Jacobs. We will be staying at his house while we visit."

"It's nice to meet you, Mr. Jacobs," Leah said very politely.

Trent squatted to address Leah on her level. "Pleasure's all mine, but please call me Trent."

She giggled, the dusting of freckles across her nose seeming to sparkle with her charm. "Okay, Mr. Trent."

Kane watched the little bundle of energy bounce directly into Madison's waiting arms. Leah's curly, sandy brown hair brushed her shoulders with each move. His gaze drifted to Trent, recalling their conversations the night before and thinking about how Craig paid the family debt by marrying Penelope. Madison would make an ideal wife for Craig and a perfect mother to Leah. It was clear she already loved them both so much. He only hoped his brother would act on his attraction sooner rather than later, or he just might lose her.

After shifting Leah higher on her hip, Madison shook his friend's hand. "It's nice to meet you. I can see why you live here. Fresh air and wide open space, with the bluest skies I've ever seen."

Movement caught Kane's eye, his gaze shifting as if to follow the delicate scent of lavender and vanilla wafting over. Annika approached, a smile spreading across her face as she stopped in front of the group.

"Hi Annika, it's nice to see you again." Kane pulled her large tote bag off her shoulder, his fingers lightly trailing down her bare arm as he did so. The contact sent a wave of heat through his body, his groin tightening. Despite how much he liked the softness and suppleness of her skin under his touch, the intensity of his physical reaction to Annika frustrated him. He had other things to worry about—building his business, his planned engagement to Samantha—to be preoccupied with a teenage hormonal reaction to Leah's nanny.

Madison moved next to Annika, informing everyone that she was headed back to New York.

Kane pulled Madison into a big hug. "You sure you can't stay tonight? We'd love to catch up. At least let me buy you dinner before you leave."

"You're sweet, but no. I have so much to accomplish in New York to prepare for our homecoming." Madison turned to Leah and Annika.

"You two take good care of Trent and Kane. Leah, your daddy will call you later to make sure you arrived safely. Be a good girl and remember, have fun."

Leah gave Madison a big hug. "I love you. Please take care of Daddy. He needs lots of hugs and kisses."

"I love you too." Madison turned a lovely shade of pink as she pressed a kiss onto Leah's forehead. "I promise to take care of your daddy."

As Madison turned to head back to the plane, Annika held out her hand as she squatted on her haunches in front of the little girl. "Are you ready to begin this amazing adventure with your Uncle Kane and Mr. Trent?"

"Yes!" Leah shouted. She nodded eagerly before adding, "And pizza. I'm so hungry!"

Trent laughed, winking at Leah. "I know the perfect place. How about we stop by on the way home?"

Kane grabbed Leah's other hand. Leah used the leverage to skip and jump, propelling forward. After six hops, she broke loose from her uncle and ran toward his friend. Trent led her toward his truck, kindly answering a rapid burst of pizza-related questions.

Kane turned to glance at Annika, who walked beside him. "This trip will be anything but boring. Does pizza work for you?"

Annika lifted her gaze to meet his. "Sounds great."

When they reached the truck, he stowed her bag in the back and opened the door for Annika. After making sure Leah was settled in the child seat Trent had borrowed for her, Kane took his seat, eager for the week ahead.

Leah spent the entire sixty-minute drive from Boise to Mill Creek telling them about London, her love for pizza, singing, and everything in between. Annika had tried to get her to calm down, but Kane didn't mind it. He liked experiencing the world from her perspective. A small part of him felt cheated out of a childhood; he could not remember a time growing up when he and Craig had acted so freely in front of adults.

After a while, Trent pulled the truck into a parking spot at the PB&S Café. The moment he held the restaurant door open for everyone, Kane's stomach grumbled at the smell of fresh-baked pizza, bread, and other savory delights.

Just as he moved to follow Trent inside, a male voice caught his ear. "Mr. Miller...Mr. Miller, can I have a minute of your time?"

Kane slapped Trent on the shoulder. "Will you get the table? I'll be right back."

He turned, leaving the restaurant to see who this person was and what they wanted. Aside from his family, he was not aware of who would know he was even in Mill Creek. The man was short and stocky, with round wire-framed glasses, and carried a leather notebook portfolio under one arm.

"I wanted to ask you some questions about PC Miller Corporation. I'm—"

As the man's hand went to retrieve his notebook, Kane interrupted him with an abrupt response. "All inquiries need to be directed to the public relations department."

"You can't just ignore me, that's not how this works."

Kane blew out a frustrated breath as he headed back inside the restaurant. The counter was packed with people placing orders. Leah ran up to him, tugging on his hand and pointing toward the back corner of the restaurant where a busser was clearing off an empty table.

"Who's that guy?" Trent asked.

Kane shrugged. "Someone I directed to the PCM's PR department. He's obviously confused if he thinks I have any information."

The hostess called out Trent's name and led the group back to the table. Kane pulled out Annika's chair before lifting Leah into her seat. He frowned when he realized her chin didn't reach the table.

"Kane, Leah needs a booster seat," Annika pointed out. "Will you grab one from the stack by the front door?"

He pivoted on his heel to retrieve the seat, and in a flash, the problem was solved; Leah sat at the proper height.

Trent twisted to look at the big chalkboard with the day's specials, then at the menu. "I'm thinking two large pizzas, the Mill Creek Special, and one pepperoni. How does that sound?"

"And a salad," Annika added. "Don't give me that look. We need to add in some leafy greens and vegetables."

Leah's head bobbed up and down as her focus turned to the paper kid's menu featuring animals to color and activities to complete.

Once their order was placed, Trent resumed his role as Mill Creek's travel guide, covering all the restaurants and shops in the area, along with a few local activities. "One of my favorite things to do is to fish or just have a lazy day splashing in the creek. It's supposed to be in the upper eighties tomorrow, so maybe an idea for a lazy Saturday."

Leah's head popped up. "What's a creek?"

Kane laughed and reached across the table to ruffle her hair. "It's settled. We must spend a day at the creek and show you. Does that work for you, Annika?"

"That sounds great!"

Kane lifted his glass and waited until everyone followed suit. "To an amazing week of fun! I love you, Leah."

Because Leah loved the idea so much, he had the feeling that he may have started a new tradition

The server arrived with their salad and soon after their pizzas. Annika passed out plates to everyone and loaded every plate with a serving. The table fell silent as everyone enjoyed the meal. It was not New York pizza, but it was very good.

Kane glanced over at Leah, who had tomato sauce smeared around her lips. When he tried to get Leah to use her napkin, to his shock, she wiped the mess on her sleeve. The adults laughed at the mess she made, but nothing deterred Leah from eating away at her second slice.

When the waitress dropped off the check, Annika asked, "How much do I owe you for my portion?"

"Not a dime. Dinner is my treat," Kane replied. He removed a black credit card from his wallet.

"I appreciate it. I'll start working on a market list for the week. Leah will need apple juice and snacks. I can meal plan for everyone or just focus on Leah and me—just let me know."

"We can discuss it tomorrow at breakfast," Kane said, accepting the black folio from the server and finalizing his tab. As they exited the restaurant, he paused to see if the man from before was still around. It was the first time he had ever been approached regarding PCM business, and he could not place why what the man said rubbed him the wrong way.

Seven

Annika's eyes flew open. The room was dimly lit by moonlight streaming through the gap in the drapes. Her heartbeat pounded against her breastbone. Her breathing labored as she tried to make sense of everything around her. Yesterday's events trickled into focus until she realized she was lying in Trent's guest room. She blew out a shaky breath, glancing at the alarm clock on the bedside table.

It was barely past two in the morning.

She plopped back down on the bed, fighting the blankets and her pillows as she tried to fall back asleep. As she continued to settle, she realized that her throat was now dry from the exertion of that nightmare. She tossed the bedcovers back and made her way to the bedroom door. Realizing she was only wearing a tank top and a pair of boxer shorts, she stuck her head out into the hallway to listen for signs of activity.

Satisfied that she was alone, she padded into the kitchen. Once there, she headed straight to the refrigerator, pulling the door open. The bright light temporarily blinded her. She squinted until her eyes adjusted to the light, then grabbed the carton of milk.

"You can't sleep either?" A deep masculine voice from behind startled her, causing her to drop the carton.

With a scream lodged in her throat, she moved like a spooked rabbit. She positioned her body behind the big door until she realized it was only Kane.

"You scared the crap out of me," she yelped.

He put his hands up. "I'm so sorry, I didn't mean to startle you. Let me pick up the milk." His chair scraped across the floor as he stood from the small table in the corner of the kitchen.

She bent down, retrieved the milk container, which now had a significant dent on its side, and put it back in the refrigerator. Her mind raced to process this situation. She remembered she wasn't wearing her robe and wrapped her arms protectively around herself.

"Stay," she said. "I'm fine."

"Do you need a glass?" he inquired hesitantly, remaining where he stood.

"Excuse me. I—" Annika croaked. She didn't stop until she stood behind the closed door of her room.

"Annika, wait."

She barely heard his plea. She clenched her fists at her sides and huffed.

Why did I go to the kitchen?

Mortification swamped her as heat suffused her cheeks. He'd startled her, but she also knew she could not help her reaction. His gentlemanly actions made her heart beat a little faster, although she hoped she did not make him feel like a creep.

Trent and Kane both were gentlemen, especially when they interacted with Leah, which made her heart melt. She liked having doors opened for her and being escorted by a gorgeous man. When Kane showered her with his manners, he made her feel like the most important woman in the room.

At some point, she drifted back to sleep because when she woke, she opened her eyes to the first rays of daylight. She tossed the covers off her body, leaving her cocoon of comfort behind, to head toward the bathroom. The warm water of the shower cascaded down her body while she reflected on the night before.

One day, she would stop second-guessing every action.

Tomorrow, she would handle any questions from Kane.

She finished her shower and got ready for the day, following the rich aroma of coffee. As she approached the kitchen, she felt a flash of disappointment when she realized Kane was not in the kitchen with Trent, who stood at the coffee machine preparing his cup. Trent was a handsome man. At six feet tall, she would bet that his blue eyes and all those muscles turned many ladies' heads, but Kane was who she considered sexy.

"Good morning. You're up early for a man who's supposed to be on vacation," she said.

Trent took his cup and sat at the table. "Unfortunately, my body doesn't understand the concept. Why are *you* up so early?"

"I'm working and thought it would be best for me to be up before Leah," Annika replied. "But first, I need coffee."

Trent nodded toward the coffee maker. "Cups are in the cabinet. Until we restock at the market, I can make scrambled eggs, pancakes, and bacon. How does that sound?"

"Delicious. Please tell me you like crispy bacon."

"Is there any other type?" Trent asked as he stood from the table.

"I knew you were a good man. What can I do to help?"

In a matter of seconds, Trent gave her a spatula. "I'll mix, and you flip."

It reminded her of Sunday mornings at home, where her mom would whip up a feast, while Annika usually manned the stove. Her dad always sat at the counter, drinking coffee and updating them on whatever he was reading while he waited. Afterward, he always did the dishes. The rule of the house was simple: if you cooked, you didn't do the dishes.

"You two are making the house smell good," Kane cheerfully announced as he strode into the kitchen.

Annika's thoughts disappeared the moment she saw him, freshly clean shaven. Man, did he look sexy. His hazel eyes stood out from his jet-black hair, still wet from his shower. Even the scent of his sandalwood cologne smelled good as he walked past her.

She felt some relief when he did not appear to be unnerved by her actions last night.

Trent placed a big plate of pancakes and bacon on the table. "Dig in while it's hot. I have some bacon and batter left to cook when Leah appears."

"That's very thoughtful, Trent," Annika said.

She took her seat across from Kane as Trent occupied one of the end spots. She noticed that they had both waited until she'd finished filling her plate before serving themselves. "So, are we still on for a day at the creek?"

Trent nodded. "And movie-in-the-park is tonight, too. Unless you think that's too much."

"Movie-in-the-park?" Annika asked before taking a bite of her pancakes.

Kane doused his pancakes with syrup before handing the dispenser off to Trent. "Remember the park we showed you last night, the one by the restaurant?" When Annika nodded, he continued. "The town sets up a movie screen and everyone picnics and watches a movie together."

Trent nodded in agreement. "I have blankets and folding chairs. All we would need to do is get some picnic food in town."

Annika wiped the corner of her mouth. "I think Leah would love it. You should tell her, Kane."

He grinned. "I love getting to be the super cool hero uncle. Don't forget to get a picture so I can text Craig that I'm rocking it."

Annika laughed, but it was Trent who pointed his fork in his direction. "Uh, did you even bring swim trunks or shorts in that city slicker suitcase?"

Kane rolled his eyes at his friend, but then frowned. "No, but I'm sure I can buy a pair in town. Isn't that what money and stores can do for a person?"

Trent scrubbed his hand down his face. "Good, because I'm not offering you a spare pair. I don't want your junk in my drawers."

Kane's face twisted into shock and horror at his friend's words. "I can tell from your wardrobe that you don't visit stores often enough. Maybe I should fly my tailor out to help you refine your style?"

Annika laughed even harder. She loved the banter between these two.

She had an idea that might save some time. She was pretty sure anything would look good on Kane, or even nothing at all. Her cheeks warmed at that thought.

"Geesh, you two, you don't buy something new for a creek outing. I can fix this in a jiffy," she said. Her chair scraped across the floor as she stood up. At the cutting block, she grabbed the pair of scissors and snipped at the air before she returned to stand by Kane.

"Kane, you get a free pass since you're a creek virgin. Now, are those pants special, or can you get another pair?"

Kane stared at Annika like she had lost her mind. "No, they're just custom Italian dress slacks. I can get my tailor to make another pair."

"Excellent...stand please. When I'm finished, you will have your first pair of cutoffs."

Trent roared with laughter. "I like this woman."

"You're going to cut them while I'm wearing them?" Kane's eyes were huge with confusion.

Annika squatted on her haunches in front of him. "Of course. Or if you prefer, you can remove first."

When Kane shook his head, Annika's grin widened at her victory. "Now, trust me and stand still. You'll thank me for this liberating moment. Everyone should own a pair of cutoff shorts at least once in their lifetime."

"Annika, you're my kind of people," Trent said before clearing the table.

She motioned for Kane to turn around. When he turned his back to her, she pinched the fabric above his knee. Warmth spread across her body as she trailed her hand around Kane's muscular thighs. The touch was not inappropriate as she guided the scissors around his leg, but electric sparks shot through her body, leaving her tingling all over. She was overwhelmed in the best possible way by this man.

She lifted her gaze to meet Kane's at the sound of the deep timbre of his voice. "I wonder if my tailor provides this service?"

Annika admired her work. She tapped his knee to lift his foot in order to free the discarded pant pooling at his ankle. "Not bad. Now you own the most expensive cutoff shorts west of Manhattan."

Trent tossed the dishtowel at Kane as he headed toward the hallway to load the truck. "Ah, this day is going to be fun."

Kane extended his hand to help Annika stand.

"Kane, I owe you an apology. I overreacted last night and—"

"Don't even finish that thought. You did nothing wrong. I'm sorry that I startled you." He paused for a moment, collecting himself to say more. "In truth, I also owe you an apology for being an epic ass during the interview. You are a breath of fresh air from my previous experience with nannies, and the difference caught me off guard. If do-overs exist, I claim one myself. You're perfect for Leah."

It should not matter, but his words meant a lot to her. She had forgotten how much fun she could be. She was not a victim; she was Annika Bauer.

"I appreciate that. Consider us good," she said, his words making her smile. "Okay, I should wake Leah so she can eat before we leave. This day is going to be epic."

"Good plan. Holler if you need anything."

Kane's character stood out to her. He was not pretentious, self-absorbed, or superficial. She hadn't expected someone from extreme wealth to exhibit those qualities. In fact, he seemed willing to try anything, which made her like him even more.

Would he feel the same about her if he knew all her secrets? She shoved the question aside and whispered her mantra. *I won't let one horrible experience define my future.*

KANE SAT ON THE spread-out towels in the grassy area beside the creek, a beautiful spot hidden from the main road by pine and aspen trees. He watched Leah and Annika dancing and singing something about monsters mashing while Trent had stepped away to take a call.

Never in his life had he met a woman as intriguing as Annika: complicated, intelligent, the perfect blend of sassy and sweet.

When she appeared last night in the kitchen, his brain had once again gone haywire. The refrigerator light cast a halo around her, giving him a glimpse of her rumpled hair, her shapely legs flowing to her fantastic ass, the soft curves hidden beneath her tank top. In the night, there was a vulnerability to her that he could not quite put his finger on.

And her playfulness this morning had him spinning once again. When her hand grasped his thigh as she cut away the lower section of his pants, he envisioned her delectable mouth sucking his cock, her lips curled around his shaft, drawing him deep into the velvety warmth of her mouth.

He enjoyed sex as a physical release, but their intense chemistry baffled him. He needed to stop these thoughts. Annika deserved to be treated like a lady.

His thoughts were interrupted by the sounds of laughter and water splashing. He watched Leah make a beeline toward him. At the last second, he extended his arms to receive a six-year-old child, wet and cold, who was making a beeline toward him.

"Uncle Kane, you aren't playing. Come and play with us."

Grateful for the interruption of his wayward thoughts and erotic visions, he gave his niece a bear hug. "I'll race you to the water."

Before he could blink, she raced back toward Annika, squealing the entire way.

He paused to take in the sight before him. Annika wore a one-piece suit under cut-off jean shorts and a big floppy hat. Despite the scar on her right leg, her tanned skin was flawless. The scar did not touch her beauty, inside or out, but he wondered what had happened to leave such an ugly mark behind. It added another layer of intrigue to uncover.

"He's still dry," Annika said directly to Leah, before winking at him.

Leah bent down, starting a splashing frenzy with her hands in his direction.

Not wanting to be bested by two ladies, he doubled down his efforts to splash back, and before long, they were all drenched. What a simple way to spend the day, but so much fun. There were no requirements or expectations—just four people laughing and enjoying each other's company. He felt a strange ping deep in his chest at his realization.

"How about we move toward the bank to dry off?" Kane suggested. "We need to start heading home so we can rest before movie night."

"No, I want to play," Leah whined, crossing her arms across her chest.

Kane reached down to pick up his niece, placing her on his hip before addressing her petulant behavior. "Are you pouting like a baby? I thought you were a big girl."

Leah's eyebrows knitted. "I *am* a big girl."

"Okay, so let's rewind and try this again. It's time to dry off, Leah."

"I don't want to, but I will. Can we come back?"

Kane smiled and kissed her forehead. "You bet. You know, Trent needs a big hug. Give him one before you grab your towel."

Kane put Leah down, who ran off toward his friend at full speed.

Annika giggled as she bent down to retrieve her hat that had fallen in the water. "That was dirty."

"That's what happens when you step away to take a call," Kane said as he waggled his eyebrows. "Hey, what was that strange dance you two were doing?"

Annika's eyes widened before she responded with an incredulous gasp, "The Monster Mash? You know, the song we all danced to at Halloween parties?"

"I guess I missed that one." Kane shrugged.

Annika nibbled on her lip while she studied him. "You *have* carved a pumpkin, right?"

Before Kane could respond, Annika yanked him toward her as she started to sing strange lyrics about graveyards and monsters. She radiated happiness as she twisted and turned, her legs and arms in alternating movements. It was a funny dance, but she made it sexy as hell.

"You're not moving. Dance, Kane," she said between the lyrics. "This fall, you're carving a pumpkin."

He was about to tell her that he'd hold her to that promise when she started to fall sideways. He gripped her arm, tugging her tight against his body before she hit the water. Annika's soft curves pressed against him, fitting perfectly against his taller frame. He wasn't in a hurry to let her go.

"Uh, Kane?" she asked in a throaty whisper. "You can release me now. I've got my balance back."

He released her but cupped her shoulders before she could move out of his grasp. "Thank you, Annika, for making this day special for all of us."

She nodded, surprised but still warm.

He ran his hand through his hair, giving himself a few minutes to gather his composure as she headed towards Leah and Trent. After a few minutes, he helped Trent gather the remaining items while Leah and Annika settled into the back of the truck.

"Well, it appears everyone had fun...in particular, one small fry who is snoring behind me in her car seat," Trent said over his shoulder as they made their way back to his cabin.

Kane glanced at Leah before smiling at Annika. "Nothing is better than a nap. We were fools when we were younger for protesting that sacred time."

"Damn straight," Trent replied. "So, for dinner tonight, we can grab sandwiches from the same place we had dinner last night, or I can introduce you to the best fried chicken that you'll ever eat over at the Knotty Pine Tree. It's tonight's special."

"Ooh, I love picnics. Both options sound great, so you two decide." Annika answered.

"I love peanut butter and jelly," Leah replied in a sleepy voice, rubbing her eyes with tiny fists.

Kane turned in his seat to look at his niece, whose little hand pointed at Annika's leg. "That's a big boo-boo. What happened?"

The cab went silent while everyone waited for her response.

Annika cleared her throat and shifted in her seat, placing a towel over the exposed flesh. "It *was* a big boo-boo, but it's healed now. Hey, I spy something big and green."

Giggles erupted from the backseat as Leah shouted out the answer. Kane's niece might be easily redirected, but the obvious attempt to dodge the answer told him it was more serious than an accident. He exchanged a knowing look with his friend before turning to gaze out the passenger window.

A protective instinct took root in his gut. He wanted to earn her trust with every fiber of his being. He wanted to be the person she would turn to when it mattered. Would she ever trust him enough to tell him what happened?

Eight

ANNIKA WAS IMPRESSED WITH the crowd size as the residents walked toward the park, their hands full of picnic gear. She instantly liked the feel of this town. People were friendly. The vibrant, happy vibe was infectious. The downtown area looked like it came right out of a Hallmark movie. Every storefront had been decorated, and every light pole or street sign had a basket for flowers hanging from it.

Annika couldn't think of a better way to spend a Saturday night. Today had been fun, and her body still tingled with joy from spending the day with Kane, Leah, and Trent. She also had to admit that whenever Kane had touched her, arousal flared to life. They shared a mutual attraction—she'd felt his erection when she had lost her balance earlier. She knew there could be no romantic entanglements, but that didn't stop her from daydreaming all the same. She did not have a vibrator, but maybe she needed to purchase one. How long had it been since she felt this carefree and happy?

As they walked toward PB&S Café, having decided to save the fried chicken dinner for another night, Leah talked nonstop, asking question after question about Mill Creek. Once they reached the cafe, Kane held open the door for everyone.

Before she could enter, her cell phone trilled. Glancing at the screen, she noticed it was the agency calling. "Kane, I need to take this call.

Surprise me with a sandwich, but make sure to include fruit or salad. I'll pay you back."

She swiped the bar to the right to accept the call. "Hello, this is Annika."

"It's Nancy. I wanted to reach out to see how the assignment was going."

"Everything is going really well! Leah is still adjusting to the time zone difference, but other than that, no issues," she answered.

"Excellent, that is what we like to hear," Nancy said. "And how are you doing? Any regrets or concerns?"

"Not one. I'm grateful you assigned me." A bubble of happiness swelled in her chest.

"That's great news." Nancy seemed relieved. "Well, if anything changes, give me a call. Keep up the good work and make the agency proud, Annika."

She had barely stashed her phone in her bag, turning to enter the restaurant, when a hand grabbed her arm. Dread replaced all of her excitement. She yanked her arm just as a deep growl erupted from behind her.

"Take your fucking hand off her," Kane growled. "Sweetheart, come and stand behind me."

Her panic dropped the moment his voice washed over her body. As soon as she moved behind him, he reached out for her hand.

The man who had accosted her shouted. "Is PC Miller Corporation going to take accountability for costing a man his ranch and life? I told you I wasn't going—"

"As I stated before, contact the PR department," Kane bit out. "You have thirty seconds to disappear, or I'll have you arrested for assault. If you ever touch this woman or anyone in my family again, I'll destroy you in court."

"Kane, is there a problem?" Trent asked as he approached.

"There might be if this guy doesn't leave us all alone. He put his hands on her," Kane informed his friend.

"I was only trying to get her attention." The man stood his ground. "I'm Melvin Wilcox, an investigative reporter from the *Billings Daily News*. I'm following up on a story about a potential cover-up involving PC Miller Corporation."

Kane started to respond, but Trent halted him with his hand. "I'm Sheriff Jacobs. Mr. Miller has previously told you to contact the PR department. Now, there's a fine line between gaining someone's attention and assault. Should we see what the security camera recorded?"

The man opened his mouth to respond, then closed it. "I guess I'll be contacting the PR department. If you change your mind about talking, here's my card."

Kane looked at the card before stuffing it into his pocket. Once the reporter left, he turned to Annika, searching her face for answers. "Are you okay?"

Am I okay?

Yes. That man had not been her stalker. Only a reporter who pushed a little too hard.

"I am. Thank you." She squeezed his hand. When he let go, she missed the connection and the warmth of his touch. Her heart started to beat faster for an entirely different reason. He had her back, and that made her feel cherished.

Trent met her at the door while Kane turned away to call Craig with an update. "Leah's inside with Lauren. Let's wrap up our order so that we can claim our patch of grass for the movie."

Annika really liked PB&S's farmhouse-style décor. The wooden tables, dotted with flowers in antique milk bottles, and mix-and-match metal chairs took up most of the space. The chalkboard menu that hung over the counter added a perfect touch of cuteness.

"Hey, Lauren, I'm sorry about that interruption," Trent explained as he moved closer to the counter. "This is Annika."

"Hi, it's nice to meet you." Lauren extended her hand. "No worries, Trent. Leah's great, she even helped me take an order."

She instantly warmed to Lauren's sweet disposition. "Being helpful is one of Leah's superpowers."

The other woman held out her tablet. "Okay, I have everyone's order but yours, Annika. What sounds good?"

Annika studied the sandwich listings before deciding on the house special: a fried green tomato, avocado, and arugula with a spritz of extra-virgin olive oil on multigrain bread.

After ten minutes, Lauren returned with their order all bagged and ready to go. As Kane paid and Trent inspected their bags, Annika waved goodbye to Lauren. Outside, she took Leah's hand into her own, wanting to keep her close.

She was again amazed at the turnout. Happy energy flowed throughout the area as people gathered with blankets, chairs, and coolers to spend their Saturday night with friends, family, and loved ones.

Trent herded them toward the crosswalk, exchanging pleasantries with everyone along the way. Finding a place right in the middle of the park, they made quick work of setting up their space. A slight breeze, tinged with the subtle scent of pine, stirred around them. The sky was streaked with orange and red from the sun's descent behind the mountains. Everything felt romantic, but there was no point in acknowledging it. Instead, she handed out the to-go boxes containing their dinners.

While they finished their meals, Leah started singing.

Annika wadded up her napkin and placed it in the box. "Kane, don't forget to tell me what I owe you for dinner."

He winked. "Nothing. You are my guest for the duration."

She gave him a side-eye glance and mouthed, *You sure?*

He nodded before turning his attention to Leah. "You ready for the princess movie?"

Leah jumped up, launching herself into her uncle's lap. "Yes."

She watched as Kane arranged his niece on his lap just as the lights went out and the title credits began to roll. Mill Creek wasn't just a place to live; it was a thriving, tight-knit community. Kane, Leah, and Trent settled right into the fold as other families got comfortable.

When the movie ended, the crowd clapped before scrambling to pack up and leave. Trent led the way back to the truck, with Kane taking up the rear. At the signal, they waited for the light to indicate it was safe to walk.

Suddenly, a loud screech startled Annika, sending chills down her spine. How had he found her?

She would not allow that bastard to hurt an innocent child. Heart hammering against her chest, her body moved into action. As hard as she could, she yanked Leah into her body, pushing them down to the ground. Annika curled herself around her charge's much smaller frame, shielding her from whatever was coming next.

The impact of the vehicle never came. She felt no pain.

Was she dead?

Instead, an insistent pair of hands had wrapped around her body, pulling and tugging her upward. "No...no, no-no," she croaked out.

"Annika...Annika...ANNIKA!" A voice called above her. "Annika. Sweetheart, you're safe. Leah's safe. Please come back to us."

She recognized that voice. Her body trembled as her eyes focused enough to see a handsome face looking down at her.

I'm safe.

"I've got you, sweetheart. Will you release Leah so Trent can pick her up?"

She nodded, trying to sit up.

"Are you hurt?" Kane asked.

"I don't think so, but where's Mike?" She jerked up straighter, her head on a swivel. Her gaze darted left and right, but all she saw was a small crowd gathered around them. "Did Trent catch him? Where is he, Kane?"

The sound of her own desperation tore at her resolve. Why did this jerk always come back and ruin a happy moment?

Fuck you, Mike. I wish you were dead.

"Who?" Kane asked before he glanced over his shoulder at Trent.

A hot tear rolled down Annika's cheek. "I-I thought that vehicle was coming for me. Oh God, where is Leah? Is she okay?"

Kane wrapped his arm around Annika before pulling her to her feet. "Leah's fine. A little rattled but perfectly fine."

"I'm okay," Leah's voice wobbled as she came right to her and wrapped tiny arms around her neck. "It was kind of scary."

Annika held her tight, "I'm so sorry that I frightened you. I wanted you to be safe."

Trent walked up to Annika and put his hand on her shoulder. "A reckless teenager ran the red light, squealing his tires. Tomorrow I will be calling his parents to have a little chat. Do you need medical care, or are you okay to go home?"

"Please take me home," Annika replied. She focused on her breathing to center her mind, body, and soul. As her body released, she realized she had a mild setback but was able to bring herself back to the present and avoided slipping back into the dark hole of her fear and misery.

During the entire ride back to Trent's cabin, her mind raced. She wasn't ashamed to be a survivor, but she needed to explain her reaction and everything she had been through. If Kane and Craig decided she wasn't the right fit for Leah, then so be it.

Fifteen minutes later, they were back at Trent's house. Annika cleared her throat as they all exited the vehicle. When they both huddled near her, she continued. "I need to speak to you both about tonight. I need to share some important pieces of information with you both."

Trent stood still with the practiced attention from many years in law enforcement, no doubt processing each word. Kane's nostrils flared, watching her with wide eyes. However, there was zero judgment in either of their gazes. For the first time in forever, she found herself wanting to tell someone all the sordid details of what she'd survived.

Her therapist would be pleased with her continued progress.

KANE WAS STILL DISTRESSED that the reporter had laid his hand on Annika. Then, when she threw her body over Leah to shield her from a perceived threat, his distress only increased. She'd risked her life to protect his niece without hesitation, leaving him humbled by her selfless actions. However, now he knew she had experienced something in her past that also spurred her strong reaction. A strong urge to soothe and protect Annika bloomed deep in his chest.

Kane carried Leah up to her bedroom and tucked her into bed. He probably should have woken her to brush her teeth, but what was one night? He turned on the nightlight and backed quietly out of the bedroom. He made his way toward the sound of voices coming from the front of the house.

"I'm making hot tea. You in?" Trent asked.

"Nah, when life seems hell-bent on passing out lemons, I'll choose to be more of a scotch man," Kane replied.

Trent busied himself with tea preparations for Annika. "Couldn't agree more. Make it two. Don't be greedy on the pour, my friend."

When everyone had their drinks, Kane sat at the table, covering Annika's hand with his. He loved how soft and warm her skin felt. "How are you doing?"

She shifted her gaze between him and Trent. "I'm fine, but I owe you both an apology for my reaction."

"No, you don't." Kane squeezed her hand before sitting back in his chair. "Annika, you put Leah's safety first before you even knew what was happening."

"Are you sure you don't want to speak to Kane alone?" Trent asked.

Annika sucked in a deep breath. While she appreciated his offer, she was ready to do this. They both needed to hear what had happened between her and Mike.

"No, I'm staying in your home, and since I'm watching his niece, you both should know. You'll have to forgive me. I haven't shared my story with anyone outside of my family, my therapist, and my legal team. Well, the agency knows too."

Kane's chest tightened. It bothered him that someone had dared to hurt her, bothered him to know they did. He would never go out of his way to harm someone, even if he thought a person deserved it. Thinking it did not mean you acted upon those thoughts.

"You can share as much or as little as you want. You control it all, every step of the way," Kane said, his voice gentle. "This is a safe space, right, Trent?"

"One hundred percent. I still have ties to the FBI, so there is always an option to open a can of whoop-ass if you find that useful."

"Noted," she said, the corner of her mouth lifting at Trent's comment. "When I was attending UCLA, studying to be a therapist, I was stalked by a man named Mike Folley."

Neither man said anything, waiting patiently.

She continued. "During my clinical lab my senior year, I was paired with a psychologist who conducted therapy with adults who had grown up and had difficult experiences in the foster care system. The group was designed to allow participants to share openly about their similar experiences together while also creating support networks outside of therapy sessions.

"Mike was one of the group participants." Feeling uneasy, she needed a moment to gather her thoughts. She stood to refill her cup of tea before returning to her seat. "I sensed early on in the study that he had started to develop an attachment to me. As his behavior towards me started to change, I should have informed my supervisor about my suspicions, but I chose to keep it to myself in a misguided attempt to prove myself as a clinician."

Annika took a deep breath, held it for a few seconds, and then exhaled slowly. She again focused on her breathing to calm her body, knowing the worst was yet to come. "The first flower arrangement arrived at my apartment about a month and a half into the study. There was no note. When the second arrangement appeared, there was a note accusing me of playing hard to get. I refused the delivery of the third one that came."

When Kane twined their fingers together, showing his support, her chest swelled with emotion. Greater powers worked in mysterious ways, and as she watched the two men sitting here with her tonight, she felt no greater proof than that. She felt safe for the first time in a long while.

"At the time, I couldn't confirm it was Mike, but my stalker didn't take the refusal well. I found the next delivery smashed outside my front door with a note that read *Do not refuse my generosity again.* I, of course, freaked and decided to tell my parents. At my parents' urging, I reported all of this to my professor, the clinical lead, and the authorities. Although the police were concerned there would be an escalation, there were no viable leads to follow. No fingerprints, not even a name from the florist."

Annika paused for a moment. She nervously circled her left thumb around her right.

"That is one of the worst parts of investigative work. You desperately want to protect and capture the person committing the crimes, but can't without evidence," Trent said.

Annika looked up at him, noting the sincerity in his eyes. "My professor met with my supervisor to review the participants' files, looking at any individuals who had a history of extreme violence. The overall sentiment was that I needed to stay alert and report any further incidents, and so, it was decided that I should stop attending the group meetings. Then, *poof*, the stalking stopped."

She sipped her tea. "Until a month or so later, when I came from school to find a huge bouquet of flowers sat on my dinette table, another note beneath it: *Oh, how I've missed you. If only rubber could be your flesh. The game is up, and you are next. You will be mine!*

"I called the police immediately, who turned my apartment upside down looking for evidence. While my neighbors hadn't seen or heard anything, the tires of my car had been slashed. I have no idea how my stalker had gained access, but the situation was becoming dangerous.

"In a matter of months, the world I felt safe in shifted to something dark and haunted. The hardest part of that whole experience is that I didn't have any control. Everyone around me was deciding what I should do next, including moving back into my parents' house to finish out the school year remotely."

Annika wiped away the tears streaming down her face, bracing for the worst part of the story. "After meeting with my professors, the day after the break-in, I was walking to the parking garage when Mike deliberately ran the signal and hit me with his car. He slammed into a street light pole, not even trying to apply the brakes. I somehow managed to avoid getting pinned between the car and the pole, but I still sustained serious injuries, including broken ribs, a punctured lung, and a fractured wrist. My leg required two surgeries to fix, which is where my ugly scar came from."

Depleted, she dropped her head into her hands.

"What happened to him, Annika?" Trent asked, his brows furrowed.

Annika lifted her head. "They found him. He's in prison now."

"Good," Trent said with a relieved sigh. "I'm very sorry you had to experience one ounce of his depravity."

"It's not something I'd wish on anyone." A look of concern crossed her face, tears spilling down her cheeks. "Do you think Craig will still be comfortable with me watching Leah?"

Kane could not take another second of seeing her upset. He pulled her body into his, holding her tight. A protective instinct over this woman roared to life. He was driven by a deep need in his soul to comfort her, to reinforce that she wasn't alone. He wanted to help her in any way possible so she could smile again. Every. Damn. Day.

He whispered against her hair, "I'm in awe of you, your strength, and determination. I know Craig will be, too. You looked after Leah first. I would like to update him on everything if that's okay with you?"

Annika lifted her head. "Yes, I figured you would. But I am glad I finally got to share my story. My therapist said this day would come." With a yawn into her hand, she added, "I'm sorry to dump and dash, but I'm exhausted. I'm going to head to bed."

Trent and Kane sat quietly while she padded away from the room.

Trent rested his head against his palm. "Wow, she's been through the wringer."

Kane let his head fall back on his shoulders, his mind whirling as he processed everything she had told them. "I want to figure out how I can ruin that asshole's life. Do you think money could buy some good retribution in prison?"

"Of course, you have the connections, but I would question who you are as a person," Trent said, his gaze sliding off into the distance for a minute before shifting knowingly back to Kane.

Kane's gaze snapped to his friend's. He could admit that something in him had changed, but didn't want to analyze his attraction to Annika. He was honored by the gift of her trust, and he vowed to do everything in his power to remain worthy of it.

"I should probably call Craig, especially before Leah mentions anything."

"See you in the morning, Kane," Trent said, then disappeared farther into his house.

Kane checked the time on his phone, quickly calculating time zones. It was ten o'clock at night here, so it was a little early in London. His brother normally got up at sunrise, but if Kane woke him up, then so be it. This shit couldn't wait. He dialed Craig's number and listened to the distinct international dial tone.

"This better be good, brother, it's very early," Craig groused. "Is Leah okay?"

"She's perfect. But we did have an incident earlier tonight that she may talk about, so I wanted you to know in advance."

Kane went through the events of the evening, from the near car accident to Annika sharing her story. "Her concern is that you may not want her to continue caring for Leah?"

"In my opinion, if anyone who protects my daughter first without hesitation, they are the right person for the job," Craig responded.

"That's what I told her. Before I let you go, there is one more situation we need to discuss," Kane said, filling Craig in on the pushy reporter who grabbed Annika. "Reporters don't normally follow me around, so this feels strange."

"Jesus, what is wrong with people? Tell Annika if she needs *anything,* all she has to do is ask."

A sudden rush of irritation had Kane shaking his head. "I'll take care of Annika. You focus on London."

"Noted, little brother." Craig paused for a minute. "But I'm not sure what that reporter is talking about. Dad is handling Montana, so let me see what I can find out. What was his name again?"

Kane pulled the business card from his pocket. "Melvin Wilcox from the Billings Daily News in Montana."

"Great. I appreciate the heads up. We'll talk soon," Craig said before the line went silent.

Kane blew out a deep breath, lacing his fingers to cradle his head. His mind swirled with a long list of things he had to do, calls he had to make, next steps for his follow-up project in New York, and strategizing how to get his father to drop the stupid notion of an arranged marriage to Samantha.

And now taking care of Annika. He could not get her out of his damn head.

He lifted his head when he heard the distinct sound of soft footsteps coming closer to him.

"I'm sorry to disturb your quiet space. I just needed a glass of water to take some ibuprofen," Annika said on her way to the cabinet to retrieve a glass.

"You're not disturbing me," he said, spinning around in his chair to watch her.

Her robe was tied at the waist, but her feet, aside from the peach nail polish on her toenails, were bare. After filling her glass with water from the tap, she spun on her heel to head back to her room.

As if on autopilot, he reached out to touch her arm, pleased when she stopped to look at him. "I told Craig everything, and he is in agreement with me that you are the *right* person for this job."

There was that smile again, the one that made him feel ready to do anything for her just to see it.

He slid his hand down until he circled her wrist. He stood as she stepped closer to him, moving his hand upward until he cupped her cheeks. "You're spectacular, Annika Bauer. I've never met anyone fiercer, braver, or more resilient, but the vulnerability of what you shared, it's ... Your trust is a gift."

When she didn't pull away, he added, "Though, I do want to throttle the bastard."

Her brown eyes widened, the tip of her pink tongue darting out to lick her lips right before her teeth sank into her bottom lip. "I'm not going to lie... I like how protective you are."

He emitted a low grumble. "If we're being honest, then I desperately want to kiss you." She put her glass on the table and lifted on her toes, pressing a kiss to his lips. Her lips were soft with the subtle taste of mint from her toothpaste.

He loved her bold action. He slid one hand through her hair to cradle her head and wrapped the other around her back to anchor her to him. He delved deeper into her mouth; their tongues explored each other. The world faded away in the exhilaration of contact and shared breath. His lips tingled when the kiss ended, but God help him, he wanted more.

She pressed her fingers against her lips and whispered, "Good night, Kane."

He stood alone, grinning like a teenager, like this was the best night of his life. He never realized that one mind-blowing kiss could alter his universe. Now that he did, he was truly fucked.

Nine

THE NEXT DAY, ANNIKA sat in a folding chair along the bank of the creek, listening to Leah's chatter echo through the air. She smiled at the little girl's determination to teach her doll to make mud pies. She loved Sundays. Growing up they meant her father's pancake batter hitting the griddle at seven a.m., and the whole house smelled of butter and maple before anyone changed out of pajamas. After breakfast, they'd pile into the car for whatever adventure her parents had planned: the beach to build sandcastles, the boardwalk to fly kites.

She missed those simple times. She wondered if she would ever have a family of her own to continue this tradition. The thought caught her off guard. Since her attack, she had never daydreamed, let alone thought about what she wanted in the future. Maybe it was the toe-curling kiss she had shared with Kane last night, the one that had her body craving more of his touch, that had awakened those hopes. The attraction between them drove her crazy.

Kane surprised her in more ways than one. She had no insight into his wealthy lifestyle, but he was down-to-earth, considerate, and willing to roll up his sleeves to pitch in on any task. Not only was he ridiculously handsome, but she loved his sense of humor and loyalty to his family and friends. He was a natural paternal figure with Leah; someday, he would make a wonderful father.

What did she even have to offer this spectacular man? She lived modestly and was as plain as could be. Did she dare to share these thoughts with her mom?

She clutched her phone to her chest.

On the third ring, her mother's cheery voice filled the line. "Ah, my favorite daughter, what's up?"

"I'm your only one, so I'd better be the favorite."

Her mother's laughter made her feel weightless while the sun warmed her face. This was how their interactions used to be before the accident. Today, she felt normal and alive, which made her giddy. "I wanted to check in and tell you that this assignment is going very well."

"I figured since I hadn't heard from you. Which, honestly, dear, makes me very happy. So, how is it being a nanny for such a wealthy family?"

"There are zero words to describe it, Mom. Like nada. Leah is a handful in the best way possible. She is so full of life that it makes my heart sing. Trent is wonderful and Kane...is amazing."

She informed her mom about everything that occurred while she was in Idaho, including her choice to share what happened last night.

When she finished, she heard her mom take a deep breath. "Annika, that's wonderful. How did it feel to share?"

Annika twirled a piece of hair around her finger and thought about her answer. It was the same one she had come to yesterday. "It will never be my favorite topic of discussion, but I also didn't feel compelled to hide from it either. I wanted to share it."

"My dear Annika, I'm so proud of you." She heard her mother sniffle on the other end of the line. Her words hung in the air for a moment. Annika could feel her mother's embrace over the phone as if she stood in front of her right now. "So, tell me more about Kane. It sounds like my daughter might be smitten with him."

She appreciated how her mother picked up on everything. "He's gorgeous and kind, and when he's around, everything just feels better. But I'm working for his family. My feelings feel so wrong."

"You can't help it when someone who might matter crosses your path. If this man is worthy and his intentions are sound, then he'll be open to a conversation about those concerns. Don't waste the opportunity while you have it."

"Geez, Mom, that seems rather bold. I don't know how he feels." Annika flushed.

"Exactly, dear. Give yourself permission to explore, to live, and to love. Grab the bull by the horns."

Annika rolled her eyes playfully. "It's a good thing you don't have a career in greeting cards. I'm just thinking out loud at this point, but I hear you. Please don't tell Dad."

"I make no promises, dear, but I won't bring it up," her mother offered. "I love you, Annika."

"Love you, Mom." When she hung up, she smiled at Leah, who was squatting in front of her, covered from head to toe in mud. It was on her clothing, hands, and even a few smears on her face.

Leah's eyes radiated sheer joy, making her laugh as she lined out four pies. "Look at these. I made them for my party."

Annika swiped open the camera on her phone. "Spectacular, Leah! Let me take a picture to send to your dad."

Leah's whole face brightened just before twisting into a frown. "Daddy's going to miss my party."

"Yes, but he can see what you made. When you get home, you can have another party just for him."

Her little smile sprang back into place. "And Madison."

"Exactly. Now let's take some pictures."

"What are you two up to besides making a huge mess?" Kane called out loudly as he approached.

Leah bolted toward Kane, carrying one of her creations. "We're making pies for our tea party."

Annika could not help but laugh at the puzzled look that covered Kane's face. She watched him take in the muddy little girl he held, who was getting mud on his dress slacks and oxford shirt. She walked toward the pair of them, winking at him.

"You've never heard of mud pies? It's a time-honored tradition for most little girls. Leah, will you put your pies on that tray so that we can carry them back to the house?"

Leah nodded emphatically as Kane put her back on the ground. She loaded her homemade delights and dashed toward the house where they had set up a table outside earlier for their party.

"A party with mud pies. My mother will be horrified. I think I'll snap a few pictures to send to her. It'll give her something to hold over Craig's head awhile." Kane's lip quirked before he waggled his eyebrows at Annika.

Annika shook her head. "Poor Craig. You're the pesky little brother, aren't you?"

"Of course." He beamed proudly. "This will keep Mom off my back for a good long time. I can almost hear her distress now."

"The good news is that you're never too old to be a child. I think you should make one just to say you did. You know...to be the cool uncle." And in that moment, she realized she could offer him another chance at his childhood, to fill in some of the fun parts he missed.

"These are only for show and not expected to be eaten, right?" Kane asked, holding onto the hand she offered.

"Eww...that's gross. Mud should never be consumed." Annika replied.

Kane unbuttoned his cuffs on his long-sleeved shirt before rolling them up to his elbows. He made such a simple act so sexy.

She tucked this moment away to fantasize about later. Her desire for this man was unyielding.

Annika squatted down near the makeshift work area she'd set up for Leah. "Okay, Mud Pie 101."

She motioned for Kane to follow. As she sat down next to her, his skin touching hers, electric sparks pulsed throughout her body. Was this what happened when people found their soulmates?

Shaking her head to dislodge those thoughts, she turned back to the task at hand. She twisted his palms upward and plopped a big handful of mud from the stream into his palms. "Work that glob into the pie container. Press it firmly into the pan all the way to the corners. When you finish forming the pie, decorate the top leaves, twigs, flowers, and rocks."

"The mud is silkier than I imagined," Kane stated as his skilled fingers worked through the mud.

She caught a glimpse of both the boy and the architect. She smiled as she watched him incorporate wildflowers into his masterpiece. Several drips of muddy water slid from his wrist onto his pants, making him even sexier. "You could have a career as a mud pie maker. Leah is going to love it."

"Nah, this one is just for you," he said, his voice low and husky.

"It's beautiful, Kane," she responded, accepting his gift. When she lifted her gaze to his, his lips were almost touching her. Her heart rate increased.

"Your mother would flip out if she saw this picture," Trent called, interrupting them.

She rushed to stand, disappointed. She wanted that kiss.

Kane's middle finger curled upward as he watched Trent tuck his phone away in his pants. "You have lousy timing. Delete that photo. I've already claimed that experience for Craig and Mommy Dearest."

"What is the deal with your mom?" Annika finally asked.

"She's a mother in title only. Everything she does always comes down to how the public sees or reacts to the Miller Family," Kane explained as if he were describing his favorite sandwich.

She bristled. "What?"

Trent said, "She is a vile woman who only worries about herself and her obligations to his father."

She was simultaneously shocked and angry at once. She couldn't imagine life without her mother's warmth and love. As she got a better understanding of Kane's childhood, she had only more questions.

Her phone rang, drawing her attention away from Kane and Trent. She stiffened, her breath lodging in her throat. "I'm so sorry, Kane. I need to take this call."

When she finished her call and turned around, she met two sets of very intense gazes.

Tension radiated off Kane, who spoke first. "Are you okay? What's happened?"

"It's okay. It was the lead detective who worked my case in LA. Some of the evidence they collected during the investigation is ready for me to claim, but my lawyer can get it."

"A call like that can be jarring," Trent said.

Annika nodded, then took a deep breath. "It's part of the process."

Kane pulled her into his side. "Are you ready to get this tea party started?"

She appreciated the change of topic and began moving toward the house. There was nothing further to say. She made a mental note to reach out to her lawyer and instruct him to throw it all away.

When they arrived, Leah bounced in her seat, ready to host her first tea. Trent and Kane both bowed to Leah before taking their seats at the table. As they celebrated, they took several pictures to mark the occasion, including a photo of Leah sitting between Annika and her uncle, to share with Craig. Although the whole affair lasted only a few minutes, Leah beamed with happiness.

Once they had cleaned up after the party, Annika excused herself to start dinner and set the mudpie Kane had made for her on the kitchen windowsill. Figuring a hot dog and s'mores roast would be easy and fun for everyone, she assigned setting up the fire pit to Kane and Trent while she and Leah made her mother's homemade potato salad.

As she slid the peeler over the brown skin of the potato, the screen door clattered. Kane entered the kitchen, his body heat enveloping her frame as he stood directly behind her. He stood as close as he could without touching her, and all she wanted to do was press herself against him. Oh, she had never desired anyone in her life like she did this man.

She forced herself to concentrate on her task, grabbing another potato to peel. "Did you need something?"

"Aluminum foil. I think it's in the drawer next to you."

She turned sideways to give him room to open the drawer. Now they were facing each other with the slightest gap between them.

"You look pretty good in mud, Kane. Please share those pictures—"

She did not finish what she was saying because Kane chose that moment to lean down and press his lips to hers. Her body shouted *hell yeah* while her brain short-circuited; instead of pulling away, she kissed him back. Annika felt his hands winding around her waist as he pulled her flush against his body to devour her lips. Every nerve ending in her body sang *hallelujah.* Just as the kiss started to deepen, a little voice shouted from outside the screen door, causing them to pull back from each other.

"Wasn't my party fun, Uncle Kane?"

Annika heard the slight groan escaping his lips as he turned to greet his niece. "It was the best. Madison will be impressed with your party planning."

Leah's smile spread across her little face before she moved toward Kane to give him a big hug. As she pulled back, she turned towards Annika, "I'm ready to cook poto salad."

Annika blew out a quick breath. This precious child had rotten timing... or maybe it was perfect timing. What had she been thinking?

She grabbed the stool and set it beside the sink for Leah. "It's *potato* salad," she corrected.

Her lips tingled from his mind-blowing kisses. Her body became hyperaware whenever he was near her. She giggled as her mother's words echoed in her mind. *Grab the bull by the horns.*

It was time to talk to Kane.

After dinner, Annika and Leah went inside to watch a movie. Kane had no doubt that she was giving him time to spend with his friend, but oddly, he missed her presence. He liked so many things about her. Their conversations felt authentic, never revolving around gossiping or brownnosing to get an invite to the next gala. And then there was the intensity of their mutual attraction. When he kissed Annika in the kitchen, he was harder than a rock.

He ran his hand through his hair. He needed to figure out a way to stop his father's plan of having him marry Samantha.

Kane twisted his head to look at Trent, who was working to put the fire out by adding dirt and raking the coals. He was deep in the silent, brooding reflection he did these days.

"You okay?" Kane asked.

He watched as his friend tucked away whatever occupied his thoughts and slowly made his way back to sit next to Kane. "A better question is, do you have anything you want to confess?"

"I wasn't aware that I had sinned. Or that you were Catholic, for that matter," Kane challenged him.

Trent chuckled. "You can try to avoid this subject all you want, but there's a certain nanny who's caught your eye. So, do you have the balls to go after what *you* want?"

Kane was caught off guard. He wasn't aware that his actions and feelings toward Annika were that transparent. "If you're judging, glance in the mirror. You've owned that crown since you lost your partner. You've shoved almost everyone away and won't talk about it."

Trent glowered at him.

They sat in prolonged silence. Kane didn't want to fight with Trent, but he was worried about him. His friend was holding onto his demons until he inevitably imploded.

"Look, at some point, Trent, you're going to have to deal with it," Kane stated on a frustrated sigh.

"I know, but today isn't that day," Trent replied in a flat tone.

"I don't want Annika to go," Kane said, taking that as his sign to change the subject. "My father is going to have to find an alternate way to accomplish his goals. My life isn't a bargaining chip he gets to play."

"Good because I like her. Since I'm stuck with you, I'd rather have you happy."

Kane groaned. "You're making me blush. I'm at least doing something about it."

"Jesus, you're like a dog with a bone," Trent grumbled. He stood, patting Kane's arm. "I'm beat. I'll see you in the morning."

After seeing all that his parents had endured and what Craig had experienced, Kane knew he was making the right decision. The hardest part would be convincing his father, but he would.

Kane's phone vibrated. He tugged it free, seeing a text message from Larry.

Call me ASAP.

His friend picked up on the first ring. "Sorry to bother you while you're out of town, but I uncovered and confirmed an interesting bit of information from the bank earlier today."

His chest tightened at the seriousness of his friend's tone. "What's up?"

"I was able to confirm that not only did both of our fathers meet with the branch manager a few days before your signing, but the loan officer confirmed there were no *formal* conditions appended to your file. When you signed the document changing PCM to be the principal on the loan, you unknowingly accepted the outcome."

"Are you saying my dad deliberately fucked me?"

"Yes. And my dad was complicit in this scheme." Larry's voice trailed off. "It's unethical."

Fucking hell.

Acid churned in Kane's stomach. He had thought his dad was jumping in to help him. This was so much worse. His father manufactured this whole damn thing.

Fuck you, Dad.

"I need time to process this. In the meantime, keep this between us." Kane terminated the call.

Frustration expanded in his head and chest. He rubbed his hand through his hair again and exhaled, trying to breathe through the discomfort building in his body. Larry's update stung.

He itched to call Craig, but he did not want to burden him with his trivial problems. He knew that as soon as he told him, Craig would jump into the fight. He had always been the buffer between Kane and their father, defusing their father's negative reaction in every situation.

Kane padded down the hallway toward his room. Just as he sat down on the bed to remove his shoes, his phone rang.

He snatched it up. "Hello," he gritted out.

"Son, I need you back in New York tomorrow." The moment Kane heard his father's voice, he realized his mistake in not checking the number of the incoming call.

Kane inhaled deeply, holding it for a few seconds before releasing it. He needed to control his anger because attacking his father would serve no purpose other than the fleeting moment of satisfaction. Although he was irritated, he knew he would use this meeting to discuss that he had no intention of marrying Samantha.

"This is rather late notice, but I'll see what I can do," Kane replied, his voice devoid of any emotion.

"I've already sent the plane. Be ready to depart tomorrow at nine a.m. Once you land, you will meet me at my office, and then we will have dinner to attend."

The line died. How typical, ending on an edict, not even a goodbye from his father. Well, his dear old dad wouldn't like his messaging tomorrow. Just as his father had taught him years ago, he needed to figure out his father's vulnerability so he could exploit it. There was a reason behind this marriage.

Ten

TIRED OF TOSSING AND turning the night before, Kane sat in the kitchen working on his laptop. As he continued working, Samantha called.

"Hey!" she greeted, making him smile.

"Hey, it's early. Is everything okay?"

"Not sure yet, but I wanted to let you know that the legal paperwork is ready for me to review. Well, for my father to review. Apparently, I continue to have little say in the matter. Anyway, I'm supposed to meet my dad at some lawyer's office in New York today."

Kane now had an idea about what this meeting was about. "Behr & Goldstein?"

"Yeah, that's the one."

"I've also been summoned by my father to meet in New York." Kane paused, trying to think. "As you review the documents, mark anything you dislike or want to challenge. That will create tension and help delay the process. Don't worry. We still have time to stop this."

"Okay. I'll do whatever I can to make all this stop."

"Trust me, I'm motivated too. Thanks for the heads up, Sam."

Kane stood to watch the sunrise out the kitchen window, drinking his coffee slowly. He really did love it here. It was so beautiful and peaceful being in the mountains. He continued to mull over how he would approach his father today.

"It's awfully early to look that serious," Annika said as she entered the kitchen.

"My presence has been requested in New York today," Kane responded sourly. "Will you be alright watching Leah on your own? I will be back tomorrow afternoon."

Annika's eyebrows bunched for a moment. "Yeah, absolutely. Is everything okay? That seems like a lot of travel for a quick meeting."

"That's my father," he said with a sigh.

"Madison had mentioned that your father could be demanding." Annika poured herself a cup before joining him at the table.

"My father's time is consumed by running a global conglomerate, while my mother's time is divided between social engagements and charities," he explained. Kane leaned back, stretching his arms. As she added sugar to her mug, he studied how her lips moved as she savored the feeling. "Thankfully, Craig and I have Linda and Albert to thank for teaching us about unconditional love."

"Who are Linda and Albert?"

Kane's thoughts briefly drifted back to his childhood. Most of his happiest memories involved Craig, Albert, and Linda spending time together. Although he never understood why his parents were unable to love them, he preferred the affection from Albert and Linda. He could count on them to listen to his problems and provide insight, to make him feel protected and worthy. With them, he felt as if he mattered rather than a pawn to be maneuvered when he served a purpose.

"Albert was my father's personal chauffeur. Linda is his wife. Honestly, they are the ones who made me a better man."

"Did your parents know how you felt about them?" she asked. Her eyes narrowed, waiting for his reply.

He shook his head and snorted. "God, no! Albert would have been fired immediately. We all knew that."

Annika frowned. "That's a horrible way to treat someone who served your family so faithfully. I would think you'd want your children surrounded by people who made a positive impact on their lives, not fire them for it."

"Agreed, which is why Craig and I hired Albert as our personal driver when our father terminated him."

She slid her hand across the table until she touched his. "For what it's worth, I appreciate the person you've become. If I ever meet Albert and Linda, I'm giving them a hug. I'm grateful they were part of your life."

He loved how passionate and unafraid she was about sharing her opinions. She would make a fierce and loving mom one day. God help anyone who dared to give her children a hard time.

"My father is not a warm man," Kane explained. "He's the product of his upbringing, where his father felt that the only way to lead your family was through tight control. Love was never part of the equation, and children were born into the family to further the family business."

"Kane, that's not an excuse. People can change. No one is perfect, but you must be willing to try," Annika replied, her gaze holding his for several seconds.

Then she stood. "I didn't mean to overstep. You're amazing, and you deserve so much more from your parents. I understand what I'm saying isn't simple, but you should do what makes you happy, not what makes your father happy."

Kane's heart nearly burst inside his chest. She made him feel like he could conquer the world and never fail. This magnificent woman accepted him wholeheartedly, regardless of his family name or money.

She was so direct and cheerful, never playing games or trying to deploy social strategy when they were together.

Kane broke eye contact first to check the time. The car he ordered would be here any minute. He reached out his arm, tugging her flush against his body. She was a perfect fit, all her soft curves feeling good.

"I'd love to see the city through your eyes," she said.

"I'd like to spend the day giving you the grand architectural tour of New York," he whispered against the crown of her head. He tilted his head down further and pressed his lips against hers. He needed a taste of her sweetness. Something he could cling to until he returned to her. He felt her body press against his as she kissed him back, his cock hardening. Their tongues dueled as their kiss deepened. It was intoxicating and exciting. Kissing her didn't whet his appetite. Instead, it awakened his inner beast, hungry for more.

He broke the kiss when he heard the crunch of gravel, knowing his car had arrived.

Her sweet smile melted his heart.

"I've got to head out," he said. "But I forgot to tell you that dinner last night may have been fun, but that dessert was epic. I missed out on s'mores as a child, but now s'mores will always remind me of you."

He watched her face flush as her eyes sparkled with amusement. "You really didn't have a childhood, so I've made it my mission to orient you to time-honored traditions."

He couldn't help but laugh. Trent would agree with her. "I'm looking forward to it."

He placed his laptop back into his designer briefcase, straightened his tie, and grabbed his jacket from the back of the chair. He pressed one more kiss to her lips before heading out to meet the driver. "Now, call me if you need anything."

KANE GROANED AS THE elevator doors slid open to reveal his father's young assistant once again. He followed her into his old man's office, where Bruce sat on one of the two sofas, finishing up a phone call. While he waited for his father, his cell phone vibrated in his pocket. He saw that Trent was calling and made a note to return his call after this meeting.

Once his dad hung up, he started the meeting without preamble. "Walter dropped off the legal paperwork. I've reviewed and approved it; all that is needed now is your signature."

Kane noticed the manila folder on the coffee table, with "*Behr & Goldstein*" printed on the outside.

"There must be another solution other than this arranged marriage," Kane said.

His father's jaw tensed, but he remained silent for several seconds. "Being a member of this family comes with endless demands."

"I understand, but this is excessive," Kane said, leaning forward with his elbows on his knees. "Break the cycle and have Walter draft a detailed agreement between you and the Secretary of the Interior instead."

His father was unmoved. "There is no cycle to break. This marriage is going to happen, son. Samantha and her father are at Walter's firm right now reviewing and signing the documents."

"The marriage between Penelope and Craig was an abysmal failure."

His father glared at him. "That situation was handled. These new contracts have been strengthened to protect us."

"You need to find another way to accomplish your goal. I'm not marrying this woman."

His father's cheeks reddened. "You disappoint me, son. This is critical for PCM; you will marry Samantha. As long as she's financially secure, I'll have some influence over Thomas and the Department of Interior's priorities."

Kane firmly pushed the folder closer to his father. This man was delusional. "Then cut them a check and make a deal with him outside of marriage."

"Leave the strategy for the actual businessmen in this room," Bruce scoffed. "Since we've confirmed the presence of rare-earth minerals in North Dakota, I need Thomas, in his current capacity as Secretary of the Interior, to arrange a land swap with the Turtle Mountain Band of Chippewa Native Americans before he leaves to pursue a presidential run. This will be huge for PCM's profits and future opportunities."

"Wow seems like a pretty gray area, one that might not have the best optics for PCM. But what do I know? I'm only an architect." Kane leaned back into the sofa.

"Enough! Marry Samantha, or I will sell your building and buy that vacant lot you're so interested in." His father regained some of his composure. "Your mother will be joining us for dinner soon, where we will be announcing your engagement. She wants to discuss the wedding details."

"Are you serious? That can wait until everything has been signed."

"Your mother needs time to coordinate with the societal magazines and news releases to ensure the entire event is befitting of a Miller wedding."

Kane schooled his reaction, refusing to give his father the satisfaction.

"One last piece of business. You report directly to me; don't go behind my back again to discuss business with your brother. You should have told me about that reporter, not Craig."

Kane was just about to tell his father that he'd lost his mind when the door to his father's office opened, and his mother entered the room. Dressed in couture, with her hair styled to perfection, she looked beautiful as always.

"Kane, darling, it's nice to see you," his mother said as she glided toward him. She air-kissed him on the cheek before perching herself on the sofa.

"Hello, Caroline," his father said.

"How's Leah?" she asked Kane.

"She's full of energy. The nanny has been wonderful, and they are doing a lot of fun activities together."

His mother patted his leg. "Look at how much you've grown. When you were little, you complained about having all those nannies. Now, you understand the value. You must have a picture of Leah."

Kane opened his phone and scrolled through some photos until he found one he'd taken of Leah smiling at the movie-in-the-park night. He tilted his device toward his mother to show her.

"Oh my, I haven't seen her in months. She's grown," his mother replied as she snatched his phone out of his hand to study the picture up close. After several seconds, his mother started to swipe through more pictures. "Who is this?"

"Annika, the nanny Craig hired," Kane replied with his palm extended. "I'll take my phone back."

"Hmm," his mother replied. One slender finger with a mauve tip tapped another image. A tsking sound followed. What is her last name?"

Kane groaned. "It's none of your business. She's doing a great job, and Leah is happy. That's all you need to worry about."

Caroline pressed the phone to her chest. "Well, this Annika person is not a good fit. A nanny should never be young. It's inappropriate and just gives off the impression that you could be having an affair. Bruce, speak to Craig about this and have him correct this oversight."

"Stop it, Mom. I can guarantee that Craig will ignore your plea because she makes Leah happy."

His mom stood and handed the phone to his father, who studied the pictures. When he finished his review, he tossed the phone back to Kane. "I'll speak to Craig tomorrow. Caroline, let's head to dinner."

Kane sent off a quick text to Craig to forewarn him that Mom did not approve of Annika. He grabbed the folder from the coffee table and shoved it into his bag while he pressed his phone to his ear to listen to the voicemails Trent had left.

Kane, it's Trent. Call me back when you get this message.

Kane, nothing is wrong with Leah and Annika, but it's urgent that we talk. We have a situation here.

Having dinner with his parents was not high on his list of priorities for the night. What he needed was time to think and decide how he would proceed.

"Mom, Dad, something has come up that needs my immediate attention. Enjoy your dinner."

"Kane," his mother chastised.

"Leave it be, Caroline. He's sulking," Bruce said. "I'll expect those documents returned redlined or signed within seventy-two hours."

He did not stop to acknowledge either of them as he headed toward the elevator. His gut tightened with apprehension. The elevator car dinged on its descent. The lobby light illuminated the space. He stepped out onto the polished marble floor and proceeded to his car, which was waiting in the reserved parking space in front of the building.

"Albert, home please," Kane said, then called Trent back. He watched Albert maneuver the vehicle into traffic before Trent answered.

"About damn time, Kane. That reporter from the other day is dead."

Kane's mind whirled from that statement. "What?"

"My deputy on scene called this morning to inform me that a car had gone off the road on the switchbacks. The driver sustained a broken neck, but more importantly, Lance reached out because he found a picture of the three of us from that night under his seat."

"What happened?"

"Pending autopsy results, it's still under investigation. The preliminary theory is a failure to control the vehicle, since it doesn't seem that another vehicle was involved. It bothers me that the only personal effects recovered were the photo and his suitcase. We haven't found his cell phone, laptop, or any other work items."

Kane pulled the manila folder from his briefcase and set it on his lap. "How did Annika take the news?"

"She seemed more shocked than upset."

"That's good, at least. She's been through enough. I still can't believe he's dead."

"Yeah, which brings me to another point. I think you both should come down to the station to give voluntary statements since a few residents witnessed the terse exchange that night."

"Got it. I'll be back tomorrow afternoon," Kane said

"Do I dare ask how the meeting with your father went?" Trent asked cautiously.

Kane updated his friend on what Larry had discovered and how his father was pushing for a quick marriage to Samantha.

"I'm sorry, man. That's fucked up," Trent said.

"I couldn't agree more. I'm ripping the documents in half and going to see if Albert will deliver this folder to my dad's office on Thursday." He glanced up and met Albert's gaze in the rearview mirror.

Albert nodded. "It would be my pleasure, Kane."

Kane smiled and put the folder with the document in the passenger's seat. "Thanks, Albert. Okay, Trent, I'm here. I'll see you tomorrow."

The stress he had felt earlier had eased. After getting out of the car, he stared at his building, marveling at its beauty. He had left a mark on the world. It hurt that his father was willing to shred his heart and dream, but if this building was the price of his freedom, it was worth every fucking penny. Now he needed to figure out how to move forward.

Eleven

ANNIKA HEARD HER PHONE and reached around the nightstand to find it. She opened one eye to see a blurry four on her alarm clock. Her heartbeat quickened as she realized that a call this early was probably not good news.

"Hello," she answered, sitting upright and drawing her knees toward her chest.

"Miss Annika Bauer?" a male voice asked. When she acknowledged, he continued. "This is Officer Martin Rolo from the NYPD. I'm calling because your Fiat, along with several other cars in your parking lot, was broken into last night. Both your driver's and passenger's side windows were smashed. It appears the burglars were looking for valuables. Did you keep anything of value in your car?"

In an instant, she was wide awake. A tendril of dread snaked down her spine. "No, nothing except my insurance card and registration. Maybe a few other trivial items."

"Okay. I'll need you to come down to inspect your car so that we can file a report," the officer stated.

Annika scrambled to turn on the light. "I'm out of town for work at the moment."

The officer's walkie-talkie crackled with police chatter before he responded. "We can get your information over the phone, but someone will need to get your car to a shop. Is there someone locally who can help you out?"

She opened her phone's notepad app to record the officer's information. "Okay, give me a few minutes to figure something out, and I'll call you back."

Annika let her head fall back between her shoulder blades as she stared at the ceiling. Thoughts swirled in her head. Could she get a freaking break? Was this random, or could her stalker have escaped? How much would the repairs cost? Could a car even be towed without a key?

She didn't know what to do. Calling her parents was not an option. A call this early in the morning would scare and worry them. Her fingers hovered over Kane's number. She decided it made more sense to ask Trent rather than bother Kane, who was across the country in New York.

She padded down the hallway and lightly knocked on Trent's door, not wanting to startle him or wake Leah up.

The door opened faster than she had expected.

"Trent, you're up already?" she asked a fully dressed man.

He nodded. "I was about to head out for a run. What's up, Annika?"

She pointed to Leah's room. "Can we talk in the kitchen?"

"Sure," he said, following her toward the front of the house.

Once they were both in the kitchen, a slight tremor worked through her body.

"The NYPD just called me to tell me that my car was damaged. Someone smashed the windows. The officer asked if someone could help me get my car to a repair shop since I'm here. Can you even tow a car without the key? I thought you might—"

Trent grabbed both her hands and held them. "Annika, I need you to breathe. Everything is going to be okay."

The second he took her hands, the tears welling in her eyes ran down her cheeks. "Do you think he escaped?"

"No, I don't think so, but I will find out just so that you know for certain. Hold on, I'm going to call one of my friends at the FBI," Trent replied, removing his cell phone from his pocket.

She nodded. She was almost certain it was a random event with how many cars were vandalized, but it would make her feel better to know for sure. She was not going to apologize for needing the validation, but she still hated it. She practiced calming breaths while she waited for him to finish his call.

I won't let one horrible experience define my future.

"Hey, Noah, it's Trent. I'm sorry for the early call, but I need a quick favor. I have you on speakerphone with Annika Bauer. She's nannying for Craig's daughter while Leah and Kane are visiting."

"Hi, Annika," Noah said.

"Can you work your cyber god magic and access the California Department of Corrections and Rehabilitation database? I need you to verify that Mike Folley is still in prison."

"Absolutely, although throw me a hardball next time. I don't even need my superhero powers for this search," Noah said, the sound tapping keys in the background. "Got it. Yup, he's still locked up. I don't see any active alerts at his prison."

"He's locked up." She exhaled a deep breath. "I'm guessing the other piece means the prison is quiet."

Trent nodded before turning back to his phone. "Noah, you are the best! I owe you a beer, man. Thanks."

He finished up the call quickly and queued up another number on his screen. "Now, let's call Kane. He's already in the city. He can get your vehicle towed to a repair shop."

"Thank you, Trent," Annika breathed.

He passed his phone off to her. "Anytime, Annika, anytime! If you're good, I'm going to go and work up a sweat."

She waved him off and hit the call button.

"Hey, what are you doing up so early?" Kane answered.

"I hope I'm not disturbing you. I really need your help if you have a moment."

"Hold on. I was just about to jump in the shower," Kane said.

He was probably naked right now. Tingles spread across her body. She groaned inwardly and put her forehead in her hand. At least this feeling was better than the one of dread a moment ago.

"What can I do for you, sweetheart?"

Her heart melted. He did not even know what she needed, yet he was so ready to help. "My car was broken into earlier this morning, and I need to get it towed to a shop. Do you know a good repair shop? One that isn't too expensive?"

"I will find a good repair shop," he reassured her, although his voice was rougher than usual. After asking for details about her car and the case officer, he added, "I'm sorry this happened, Annika. I can't imagine how you felt getting that call."

"I'm better now. Trent checked with a friend of his to make sure my stalker was still in prison. It would be so Hollywood for him to have escaped, but I couldn't take the risk of not knowing for sure."

"I'm glad Trent could help."

She appreciated that he was supporting her, instead of giving her irritating platitudes that the ordeal was over now or that it could have been worse. Instead, he listened, asked how he could help, and stood by her side.

"Trent is a good man, although not as good as me. Don't tell him I said that," Kane teased. "I'll get this handled before I fly out, but if you need anything else, just call me."

After they hung up, Annika texted him a photo of her car along with the officer's phone number. She was looking forward to having Kane back and talking to him like her mom suggested.

Afterward, she headed back to her bedroom to get her wallet to make one more call. The sooner she could put that phone call behind her, the better.

Trent was standing at the sink, washing dishes, when Annika had finished getting ready for the day. She started getting Leah's cereal ready. "How was the run?"

"Brutal, but I shaved just a minute off my time. So, I'm happy," Trent said, flashing her a big smile. "Did you get everything squared away?"

She opened the cabinet to take out cereal, and then the next cabinet over to get a bowl. "I did. Hey, a thought occurred to me while I was showering. Does Kane understand the concept of an inexpensive repair shop, or should I have been more specific?"

Trent turned around, the kitchen towel slung over his shoulder, an even wider grin on his face. "Honestly, I think he just buys a new car when he needs a set of tires or something."

She smacked her forehead. "Great. I'd better not need a loan to get my car back when I get home."

Trent snapped the towel off his shoulder. "I would bet my next paycheck that you won't be paying a dime for any repair."

"That better not happen! I am not expecting him to pay for it."

"Trust me. He knows that, but I'll let you two work that out." Trent flashed her another knowing grin. "Hey, I've got to head into the office for a bit. Do you want me to leave my truck for you to use?"

Annika shook her head. "No, but I appreciate the offer. Do you want to join us for lunch?"

Trent grabbed his keys off the counter and a bottle of water. "Not today. I'm treating the team to pizza since everyone had a long day yesterday working on that accident."

"That's nice. I'm sure they'll appreciate it."

As he started to leave, his phone rang. Since his hands are full, he pressed the speakerphone button.

"Mr. Jacobs, this is Irene Shaw, a concerned citizen of Mill Creek. I'm calling to request a citizen's arrest. How soon until you can lock him up?"

Annika suppressed a laugh with her hand at Trent's pained expression.

"To process a citizen's arrest, you would need to witness a specific crime. Do you have any evidence to corroborate such an arrest?"

"Not exactly," Irene answered. "But nothing good ever happens after midnight. He's up at odd hours and spends a lot of time walking in his yard, staring at the ground. He can probably tell you the exact number of weeds and rocks in his yard. Normal people don't know that information."

"Irene, I know you are a vigilant resident, so how about a compromise?" Trent offered. "When I'm back from my vacation, I'll go out and introduce myself and see how he reacts to my presence."

"He could be dangerous, Sheriff," she squawked.

"Or maybe he could be adjusting to small-town living and friendly intrusions on his privacy?"

Irene huffed on the line. "Fine, but I want it on record that I'm starting a journal to track his activities. It will be in my nightstand drawer when you find my dead body. And you will have to provide a verbal apology at my funeral, Trent."

"Noted, but I don't want that to happen, because this town needs you," Trent replied.

"Flattery does go a long way. Now enjoy your vacation, sheriff," Irene said before hanging up.

A second later, Leah burst into the kitchen, making engine noises, her arms spread wide. "I'm a plane."

Trent squatted down and Leah ran right into his arms.

"Good morning, Leah." He scooped her up and set her on his hip. "Now, you're high in the sky."

Leah giggled. "Do you wanna play?"

"I've got to do some work, but how about later this afternoon?" Trent asked.

"Okay, but I may fly really far while you're gone," Leah responded, her lips vibrating from a new set of noises.

Trent turned his hand so that his first two fingers were aiming at his eyes before turning his fingers toward her eyes. "Well then, we need to keep our eyes on you."

Giggling followed.

"Fly on over here, Leah, so you can fuel your plane," Annika said.

Trent put Leah down in the chair and nodded to Annika. "Have fun, ladies. Call me if you need anything."

Annika started pouring milk into the cereal bowl. "Tell me when, Leah."

After a few splashes, Leah gave her the signal. She went to town crunching down her breakfast.

Annika said, "After breakfast, I thought we could finish our movie, and then we'll head outside for a while."

Leah wiped her mouth on the back of her hand. "Yay, I love those toys in the movie. They are funny."

After Annika finished breakfast and cleaned up the kitchen, she joined Leah in the living room.

Leah giggled as the movie ended. "I don't want it to be over. I liked it."

"That's the best part of a good show: you get to take a piece of the magic with you."

"I do?" Leah asked, her eyes wide.

"Only if you believe." Annika winked. "How about we head outside and explore?"

The day moved in slow motion. Annika checked her watch for the umpteenth time, only to see that it was only noon. Her stomach fluttered as she thought about Kane returning home later this afternoon.

A breeze played with the aspen leaves and the long grass along the creek bed. It was beautiful here, surrounded by nature and clear blue skies. She propped her feet on the wooden railing of the porch as she watched Leah play in the yard. Her little body twirled and zigzagged as she chased butterflies while singing at the top of her lungs. If only she could bottle that energy.

"I'm hungry," Leah said as she crawled into Annika's lap. "My tummy is talking to me."

"Oh no, we'd better do something. How about a tuna fish sandwich?"

"With olives and hard-boiled eggs?" Leah asked brightly.

"Is there any other way to eat tuna?" Annika wrinkled her nose as she tickled the little girl's tummy.

"When does Uncle Kane come home?"

“This afternoon,” Annika replied as she stood up, gently setting Leah down.

"Yay!" Leah jumped up and down.

Annika felt the same way.

KANE BREATHED IN THE smell of fresh pine as he stepped out of the car. A feeling of calm washed over his body, relaxing his tense muscles. He loved New York, but being back in Mill Creek felt good. A part of him craved the simplicity and happiness that he found here.

Laughter filtered out through an open window, drawing him toward the house. The briefest glimpse of his future flashed before his eyes, showing him coming home to his wife and their children in the home he had built. The thought shocked him to his core. He had never thought he would want children. Hell, he never thought he would find a woman who would make him want to marry.

He had missed Annika, and he could not wait to see her.

Kane set down his briefcase just inside the front door. He followed the sound of giggles and chatter into the living room—or what used to be the living room. The entire space was filled with chairs, blankets, and sheets draped over the top of furniture. A massive tent structure sat in the middle of the room, with laughter coming from within. It was happy chaos.

“Where is everyone?” Kane announced in a boisterous voice.

“Yay! Uncle Kane! Uncle Kane, I missed you.”

He watched a little bulge wiggle under the covers until Leah's face appeared at the opening in front of him.

"Welcome back! Come join us at Leah's home," Annika called over Leah's squeals.

"You'd better do some stretches before you crawl back here," Trent added. "Leah's house is suited for little princesses, not grown men."

"Stop complaining, Trent. This is good for you," Annika chastised him in a playful voice.

Before Kane had a chance to respond, his niece chattered excitedly. Her patience started to fade as she hopped from foot to foot. "Uncle Kane, follow me. And no shoes."

He snapped a quick photo of Leah hamming it up in front of her house to send to Craig before he happily abided.

"Hurry, Uncle Kane! You don't want to get lost."

He got down on all fours, following his niece inside the expanse of blankets. The architect in him admired the structure and left him wondering why he never thought to do this when he was Leah's age. As he worked his way toward the middle, two familiar faces came into focus, sporting goofy grins.

"Do you love it?" Leah gushed as she crawled around and sat right between Annika and Trent.

"You did a spectacular job, kiddo," Kane replied.

Leah's little face glowed with pride as she rocked back and forth on her knees. She asked Trent to take their picture while she waved Kane over to sit next to Annika.

After taking a few photos on Kane's phone, Trent said, "I'm going to stretch my legs and get a drink."

"I think you might have a little architect on your hands," Annika said as she winked at Kane.

He warmed at the thought of his niece following in his footsteps, maybe even working side by side one day. His mind struggled to grasp how vastly different Leah's childhood was from his and Craig's. While he and his brother had so many wonderful cultural and artistic experiences growing up, they missed out on the magic of imagination and play. At least Leah had the best of both worlds.

Kane answered the incoming call from Craig. "You got my pictures?"

"Yeah, it looks like Leah is having a blast," Craig replied, before yawning. "Put my little ladybug on, and then I've got an update for you."

Kane gave the phone to Leah. "Will you bring my phone to me in the kitchen when you're finished?"

She nodded emphatically and turned her attention to the phone. "Daddy, I miss you so much."

Leah gushed about everything she had been doing as he followed Annika towards the exit of the tent, watching her delectable bottom sway the entire way. When she stood and turned to offer her hand, he accepted, tugging her into his body as he stood up. He cupped her cheeks, rubbing his thumb across her bottom lip.

"You're a treasure," Kane whispered before crashing his lips down onto hers. His hands left her face to trail down her body, settling on her lower back. He pulled her closer to his muscular frame, his hardened length pressing against her abdomen. He kissed her thoroughly, touching every inch of her warm, soft mouth. He had never wanted anything, or anyone, as much as he wanted her.

Reluctantly, he pulled back and rested his forehead against hers. "I needed to remove the unpleasantness of my trip. I feel invincible when I'm with you."

Big, beautiful brown eyes gazed up at him. "That's the nicest thing anyone has ever said to me."

He slid his hand down to hold hers as they went to the kitchen, where Trent waited with three bottles of beer. After two long days, a cold one sounded great.

"I'm starving. What's for dinner?" Kane asked.

Annika said, "Wait. Before that, what happened to my car?"

"I had it towed to the Fiat dealership. Your side windows will need to be replaced, but the interior wasn't damaged. I did ask that they perform a full end-to-end check and service. Just to be safe."

"Thank you." Annika pointed to Trent, who raised both hands in the air. "And, Kane, with Trent as my witness, I'm paying you back for everything."

It had thrilled him that she trusted him enough to ask for help in the first place. He had no intention of letting her pay for any of the repairs. "We can talk once I get the final bill. So, what's for dinner?"

"We're having steaks and potatoes," Trent answered.

"I can whip together a salad and steam some broccoli," she offered.

"I'm good with the first two items," Kane said.

"Uh, we don't need the other, Annika. I'm with Kane," Trent added.

Annika put her hands on her hips. "You know the green stuff is good for you. We need to set a good example for Leah."

"What's good for me?" Leah asked, appearing in the kitchen with Kane's phone in hand.

"Fruits and vegetables, Leah," Annika said, rubbing her back.

Leah scrunched up her face, then remembered the phone she was holding. "Here, Daddy wants to talk to you."

Kane took the phone. "I'm here. What's up?" he asked Craig as Annika led Leah down the hallway for a bath.

"Firstly, thanks for the lecture from Dad on my poor choice in hiring Annika," Craig answered sourly.

Kane tossed his head back and groaned. "At least you didn't have to hear it in person. Trust me, that was worse."

"Fair enough," Craig acquiesced. "Secondly, I think I figured out what that reporter from Montana might have been investigating. It seems a local rancher sued PCM many years ago, alleging that our mine failed to properly manage the dump site, allowing waste to seep into the soil and reach the water table. According to his lawsuit, our negligence wiped out most of his cattle and caused several residents to get severely ill or, in some cases, die. The court dismissed the case due to the prosecution's lack of evidence, but I am planning to send this information to our PR department, so they're prepared if the reporter contacts them."

"I don't think that's necessary anymore," Kane said, a knot forming in his stomach. "He died in a car accident yesterday as he was leaving Mill Creek."

Craig was silent for a beat. "That's horrible. I might send it along anyway, in case his notes and files are given to another reporter. How did it go with Dad?"

Kane did not want to mislead his brother, but with how much Craig had on his overloaded plate, now was not the time to tell him about their father's marriage plot. "Typical Dad stuff. He's very focused on the library project and possibly a new one in North Dakota, but I'll fill you in later. Go get some sleep. You sound exhausted."

Kane shared with Trent what Craig told him. "Did your deputies ever find the reporter's phone or any of his work materials?"

Trent shook his head. "They found nothing. I even had a few of my deputies walk back into the tree line to see if anything might have been thrown farther from the crash site. It doesn't make sense."

"Do you think Wilcox found new evidence?" Trent asked.

Kane shrugged. "Maybe? Why else would you spend resources on a case that had been dismissed?"

Trent pointed at Kane with his empty beer bottle.

Kane nodded. "Yeah, we're gonna need another round when I tell you what happened in New York."

Trent's eyes widened. "I hope it starts with you giving your old man hell."

"You bet. Dad will know I'm not pleased once Albert delivers the ripped documents on Thursday."

Trent gave a fist pump to Kane. "I wish we could bug his office to hear him blow a gasket. I'm sorry about your building, though. He's truly a dick."

With a fresh beer in hand, Kane started. "What I'm about to share must remain between us. I live in the gray, Trent, and I don't want to put you in an awkward position."

"I can handle gray."

"The woman my father wants me to marry, Samantha, is the daughter of the current Secretary of the Interior, Thomas Monroe. I imagine this marriage is one more way he can control Monroe, but he also mentioned needing the Secretary to broker a land swap in North Dakota before he leaves office for a presidential bid."

"It's unethical, but not too shocking," Trent said, disenchantment in his voice.

"Samantha and her father were in New York, too, meeting with the lawyers to review the contracts. I told her to redline the contract to postpone the signing."

Trent's lips went flat. "Do you know if she signed the papers?"

"Not sure yet, but I'm going to call her later to see how it went."

Trent rubbed his forehead. "You've got to tell Craig."

"I do. I plan to tell him soon. I just don't have the energy tonight."

"Do you have any objections to my reaching out to Noah and having him dig into what happened in Montana? Maybe see if he can figure out why this reporter is investigating a closed case."

Kane shook his head. "No. I mean, he died in your county, so you're just doing your job."

"Exactly. Tomorrow, you and Annika need to come down and give your statements." Trent smiled as he changed the subject. "In other news, I'm ready to hire you to renovate my home. There will be a budget, Kane, but I want the best man for the job."

Kane grinned. "About damn time. I'm not giving you any discounts. I have expensive tastes."

Trent groaned dramatically.

The phone chirped with a new text message. Kane started reading Samantha's messages aloud.

Samantha: I'm still with my father, so I can't talk. I asked for two changes, but I can't leave until I sign the revised documents, which will be ready in an hour. My Dad is freaking out. I've never seen him so upset. I'm sorry. How about you?

Kane: I'm so sorry for all of this, Sam. Sign your documents, and I'll handle the rest. I ripped mine up. They'll be delivered to my father on Thursday.

His friend patted his shoulder. "I know this isn't easy, but walking away with your integrity is the right choice. I'll get Noah working."

"Sounds good." Kane took the last sip of his beer. "Let's start working on the renovation plans after we go to the station tomorrow. I'll need the diversion."

Kane grabbed his briefcase before heading to his bedroom. He should never have accepted his father's help with the loan. He walked right into his dad's trap and into this ensuing nightmare. Well, won't his father be surprised when he receives his message?

How does it feel, Dad?

Twelve

Annika folded the last shirt from the dryer when a small flash of a girl whirled past, skidding to a stop right next to her. "We have wind! Can we fly the kite you gave me?"

She ruffled her head. She motioned for Leah to follow her as they headed to the family room to look out the big windows.

There was something extraordinary and relatable about Leah's excitement. When Annika was little, her parents would take her to the beach, where she and her father would fly their kite before dipping into the ocean to cool off. Her mom was usually nearby, sitting under the umbrella, taking pictures. She loved those simple days, those memories she would forever cherish.

"You are right, Leah. Kite flying, here we come!"

Annika scribbled down their plans on a note and placed it on the refrigerator. She walked Leah to the beautiful meadow she found across from Trent's house by the babbling creek. She thought this piece of land would be perfect for a home. At the meadow, the breezes were strong, so she knew they could fly the kite high into the sky.

She opened her backpack and showed Leah how to prepare the kite for flight. As she stood to watch, she heard footsteps approaching from behind. She glanced over her shoulder to see Kane and Trent joining them in the meadow.

Since Kane had returned from New York, he and Trent had spent the last week finalizing the plans for the renovation project. Unfortunately, the general contractor was unavailable on Sunday afternoon, so they headed down to Boise early this morning to meet and, hopefully, hire him, as well as file the project permits.

Over dinner the night before, Kane had pulled out blueprints to share what Trent and he had decided to do with the cabin. She noted the plans for an expanded kitchen with a large island and the upgraded master ensuite featuring a luxurious steam shower with multi-spray heads. She enjoyed watching him in action, noting how his love of architecture was evident in every detail.

"How'd Boise go? Did you get everything finished?" Annika asked.

"We did. Now all we have to do is get the remaining supplies ordered," Kane answered.

"Uncle Kane, look, it's so high!"

"Way to go, Leah! Your kite is almost touching the clouds," Kane called out. He turned around in a circle, taking in the spot. "This meadow is breathtaking. All the wildflowers blooming, the creek in the background...this would be a perfect place to build a house."

Annika looked at Kane. "I literally just thought the same thing."

Annika squatted to give Leah a few pointers while Kane stepped away to accept a phone call. The bright yellow and black bumblebee kite zigged and zagged as it soared through the air. With each movement, the long tail undulated in the wind.

When Kane returned, he took a few pictures of Leah. "It seems my father received my package. He said I had one last chance to reverse my oversight before it's too late."

"What on earth does that mean? That sounds like a threat," Annika said in a low voice.

"That's my father, Annika," Kane said with a shrug. "I've disappointed him, so he's selling my building if I don't comply."

Annika's heart dropped. She rushed to him, enveloping him in a hug. "That's not right."

Leah shrieked. In a blink, Annika snapped her head to the right just in time to see Leah fall to the ground while her kite went wild. She released Kane as they both rushed toward Leah, leaving Trent to recover the kite.

"Leah, are you okay?" Annika asked.

Big tears rolled down her face. "I tripped over that rock and skinned my knee."

Kane squatted and lifted his niece into his strong arms, seemingly unconcerned if dirt or blood got on his designer pants. "Who's my big girl? You know, I took pictures of you to share with your father. You had that kite so high in the sky."

"It was really high," Leah said, her voice wobbling.

Annika patted her back as she walked alongside Kane. "Let's get you to the bathroom so I can clean your knee. Then, you can choose what type of Band-Aid you get to wear."

Trent had the kite in hand and motioned for Annika and Kane to go in front of him. When they reached the back porch, Kane held the door for Annika, then followed her to the bathroom.

"Thanks, Kane. We'll be out in a moment," Annika said as she gathered first aid supplies.

She went to work cleaning up Leah's knee while the little girl sang her favorite song, trying to distract herself. Pleased that Leah put on a brave face, she laid out several sizes of Band-Aids and tried not to laugh when Leah chose the biggest one for her boo-boo.

"I'm proud of you," Annika said and opened the bathroom door.

Leah ran down the hallway towards Kane to show him her bandage.

"I need to head to the station for an update," Trent said.

"Do you have to go?" Leah asked, her lips turned down.

"Yes, my assistant needs me," Trent said.

"Can I go? I could put my doll in jail. Pretty please, with frosting on top."

Trent grinned from ear to ear. "How can I refuse frosting? If Kane and Annika are okay with it, then you can all come. It won't take me very long."

A unanimous decision had them all piled into Trent's truck moments later, headed for the station. When Trent pulled them into a parking space, he turned back to look at Leah. "Are you sure you want to have your doll arrested?"

Leah hugged her doll to her chest. "Yes, but I'll be there with her."

Trent nodded and exited the truck. When he passed Kane, he grinned. "Man, Craig has his hands full with her."

As they approached Lance's desk, Trent stopped to make introductions.

"Hi, Mr. Lance. My doll is going to jail. She's bad," Leah said, placing her toy on his desk.

Kane smiled at the surprised look on Lance's face. He looked like a fish out of water, and he could relate to that feeling at first. However, with Annika by his side, he was learning a thing or two about caring for children. From previous conversations with Trent, he knew his friend really liked Lance, which meant Kane could trust Leah with him.

"Lance, will you help process Leah's doll and place her in a holding cell?" Trent directed his deputy, whose eyes were wide. "I need to meet with Aimee."

"I'm innocent! It was Lance," said a woman with bright hazel eyes and a beautiful heap of auburn hair, from behind Trent.

Trent turned around to face her. "Good to know, Aimee. Hey, I'd like you to meet Kane, Annika, and Leah. They're visiting from New York."

"It's nice to meet you, Miss Leah." Aimee dropped down to her knees. "I'm sorry to hear that your doll was naughty and is going to jail. Maybe newly uncovered information will show she's innocent."

Leah rocked her body from side to side and clapped. "I don't know."

Aimee stood and pointed at Lance. "I'll be over in a few to help. We don't want you losing your bad boy persona."

Annika instantly liked Aimee. She was a firecracker that radiated so much warmth.

Leah followed Lance toward the jailhouse, chattering nonstop and undoubtedly asking him about everything she saw.

Aimee opened the conference room door. "I just need Trent for a few minutes, but you two can hang out in here."

Annika entered the room behind Kane and took a seat. As Aimee ushered Trent away, a twinge of discomfort settled in her gut.

"What's wrong, Annika?" Kane asked, his eyebrows pinched tight.

"Nothing, it's..." Annika chewed on her bottom lip. "I guess this reminds me of when I had to deal with my stalker. You know, being in a station. Sorry."

Kane's hand covered hers. "Do you want to leave? We could go for a walk."

"No, I'm good, but thanks for the offer." Annika squeezed his hand.

"How about I distract you and tell you about what happened between my father and me when I was in New York?"

"I've been curious, but I haven't wanted to push."

She sat and listened while he shared about the arranged marriage, his father's threat to sell his building, and how PCM meant more to Bruce Miller than anyone in the family. The whole time, she kept thinking about how she wanted to punch his father right in the nose for being so callous.

She sat still, her eyes narrowed. "How can he take your building away?"

"My father believes that you need to find a person's weakness to exploit it, and KPM Towers is mine. The bank suddenly withdrew the preapproval on the day I was scheduled to sign the loan note, citing additional conditions to the loan. My father offered to intervene, in exchange for my help on three items, and then he'd transfer the title to me. Only he's the one who told the bank to withdraw the loan."

"Kane, that's horrible," Annika said, thinking about the other information he shared before moving to her next issue. "Arranged marriages sound archaic. I know there's a long history of practical or strategic marriages, but what about love? Shouldn't you be madly in love with the person you're going to marry? I mean, if it doesn't work out that way, then it might feel like a prison sentence."

"To my father, marriage is a business arrangement. He isn't concerned about love, that isn't part of his equation."

"Your father sounds like an asshole. Does this woman know her fate?"

Kane nodded. "She does. She had a boyfriend that she loves, so she isn't happy about this at all. While in New York, I tore up the prenup and marriage contracts and left a note to my father saying I'm done. He won't accept my decision gracefully, so I expect some fireworks."

"It's so cruel going after your building," Annika said, then went back to chewing on her lip.

Kane reached over and grabbed her hand. "I should have known better than to trust that his offer to help was genuine. His betrayal hurts, but it was also a wake-up call."

The creak of the conference room door had them both looking at Trent, looking serious with a folder tucked under his arm.

"I've got news," Trent said as he sat in the chair closest to Kane.

Kane turned to face him. "What's up?"

Trent put the folder on the table. "The autopsy came back for our reporter, confirming he died from a broken neck. However, based on the hemorrhaging and the tissue reaction around the fracture, it occurred perimortem. The medical examiner ruled his death a homicide."

Kane rubbed his upper lip with his fingers before he spoke. "Well, that explains why his work material was never found. Do you think that picture left in the car was a threat or a warning?"

Annika's gaze jerked up to look at the men. Her heart rate increased as she listened.

Trent sat back in his chair, folding his hands over his stomach. "No, I think it was left by accident. Over the weekend, Lance did one last check of the car and found a small thumb drive wedged between the seat rail and molded carpet. Whoever did this was in a hurry. I'm assuming the contents of his bag spilled out as they were taking it."

"What's on the drive?" Annika asked.

"It looks like a backup of his notes and research about that lawsuit against PCM's mine in Montana. I'm sending the file to Noah for review. Maybe he can find new evidence about whoever is behind this."

"Trent! Leah's on the back of some man's motorcycle," Aimee hollered into the conference room.

"What the hell?" Trent said as he sprinted from the room.

Annika's stomach dropped as the room emptied. *Please let her be okay.*

They barreled out the station's back door onto the sidewalk. A large, muscular, bald man had Leah on his motorcycle, although she didn't seem scared or in distress. Annika relaxed a little.

Trent's assistant barged ahead, stopping right in front of the big man.

"Hi, Aimee! This is my new friend, Mr. Dragon. I like his bicycle." Leah's smile brightened her whole face as she started to make motorcycle noises again.

"I'm Sheriff Trent Jacobs." Trent stepped forward, smiling at Leah before shooting the biker dude a steely stare. "It's called a motorcycle, Leah, and those are for adults. Isn't that right, Mr. Dragon?"

"I'm Clarke Dragoon. There's an extra 'o' in the name," he said in a deep voice, extending his hand to Aimee.

Aimee shook his hand. "I'm Aimee, the Sheriff's assistant."

Lance interrupted the awkward moment when everyone heard him hollering from the side of the building. "Leah, Leeaahhh, where are you hiding?"

Leah giggled, shouting back, "I'm over here, Mr. Lance."

A second later, Trent's deputy ran around the side of the building. Worry was etched on his face as he ran up to stand next to Trent. Lance's chest heaved under his uniform. "I take full responsibility. I took a call from the phone company about installing our upgraded equipment. I turned my back for a minute or two at most, and when I came back, she was gone. I'm just relieved to know she's okay."

Clarke crossed his arms over a massive chest. "I saw Leah roaming the sidewalk alone and was concerned she'd wander into the street. Or worse."

Lance winced at Clarke's comment. "I screwed up. I shouldn't have turned my back to take that call. I'm sorry."

"Lance, don't beat yourself up." Trent squeezed his deputy's shoulder. "The important part is that she's okay. Now you know that children have to be watched at all times."

"Why is everyone mad? I knew where I was the whole time," Leah pleaded as she threw her hands up in the air. "Thanks, Mr. Dragon, I had fun. If you get lonely, come over to Mr. Trent's house. We have a lot of fun."

Aimee stepped forward to remove Leah from the bike and passed her off to Kane.

"She needs the stranger danger talk," Clarke said pointedly to Kane, before waving goodbye to Leah. "She's cute but asks a crapload of questions."

Despite the fear of the moment, Annika could not help but smile at how easily Leah warmed up to people. She seemed unafraid of this big, hulking man. "Thanks, Mr. Dragoon, for keeping her safe."

Clarke started to put on his helmet when Trent asked, "Will you be staying in town for a while?"

"Not sure yet," Clarke responded. He got his motorcycle roaring to life and rode away.

Trent turned back to his staff. "I'll see you both on Monday, but you know how to reach me."

"You got it, boss. Oh! Let me go get Leah's doll," Aimee said, dashing back inside the station.

"Give me a second to send off those files to Noah, and I'll meet you at the truck," Trent said to Kane and Annika.

At Trent's truck, Kane loaded Leah into the back and closed her door before moving next to Annika. He looked at her with a pained expression. "I'm guessing I need to share this with Craig in case Leah wants a motorcycle?"

Annika chuckled. "Yes, you do. You also need to have the stranger danger conversation with her, but I'll help you with that one."

Current Day- January

Mill Creek

THE LADIES AT THE brunch shook their heads, smiling, as Annika recounted Leah's encounter with Clarke.

"Oh, my God! I swear Clarke is way too invested in this whole stranger danger thing," Maggie said, her tone showing her exasperation. "He chastised me with that same line not that long ago."

"I know." The corner of Aimee's mouth quirked up. "But he does mean well."

Maggie patted Aimee's arm. "Well, to his credit, he did save me from being killed, so I forgave him."

"I wanted to kill him so many times at the beginning. Now I do love that big, bald love machine."

Annika jumped in. "Leah saw right through his tough, crusty exterior and had him wrapped around her finger in minutes. Your giant bear of a man has a huge heart underneath all that motorcycle leather."

"Right? It took me a hot minute to see all of that," Aimee said.

"Clarke's love language is picking on people; it's part of his charm. But he is loyal. He didn't even think twice about helping Noah and me when we needed him," Jasmine added, then lifted another bottle of champagne. "Who's ready for refills?"

As Jasmine topped off everyone's drink, Maggie said, "Aimee, you were so right to be cautious at first. I can't imagine how hard Clarke had to work to get the key to your heart, considering everything you were facing."

Aimee pulled her gold locket away from her chest and pressed a kiss to it. "I'm lucky he's a stubborn man, or I could have lost him."

"We do have keepers, each one of us," Annika sighed wistfully. "Maggie, I knew Trent was a winner as soon as I met him. He had so many demons, but you helped him to see the light again."

She turned to Jasmine. "And, you, lady. Good Lord, you'll follow a lead anywhere, even into the lion's den. While none of us would be here today without his analytical and hacking genius, you freed Noah from his agony."

"I love you all." Jasmine's face glowed. "The world better watch out. Don't flipping mess with the woman or men of Mill Creek."

The girls clinked their glasses together again in an effusive show of gratitude.

"Oh! I've got to pee," Maggie said, then dashed toward the bathroom.

"Me, too! Too much champagne!" Jasmine called as she followed.

While they waited for Maggie and Jasmine to return, Aimee moved closer to Annika and wrapped her arms around her. "You are *my* hero. Not only are you brave in your life, but you were brave enough to cut Kane's designer pants right off his leg. Please tell me you have pictures. We need commemorative T-shirts."

Annika burst out into laughter. "Oh, God, he'd kill me. So, yeah, I'll send you a copy."

"What did I miss?" Maggie asked, coming back into the room.

Jasmine's voice hollered from the hallway. "Wait for me! I want to hear."

As Jasmine rushed back to her seat, Aimee showed everyone the photo of Kane wearing his custom cut-off shorts. "Girls, we're making this into a T-shirt."

"I'm going to plead innocence when Kane asks me how this got out," Annika stated.

"I don't know what you're talking about, Annika." Aimee gave her friend her best angelic face. "Now, keep going. I wanna hear how Kane explained Leah's newest obsession with Clarke's motorcycle to his brother."

June—Six Months Earlier

Mill Creek

Kane walked onto the deck and dialed his brother's number. He needed to finally fill Craig in on the finer details of his deal with their father.

"Hey," Craig answered on the first ring. "What's up?"

"Grab some scotch. This is going to be a long call." Kane sighed.

Kane started off with the easiest update, telling him about Leah's latest antics with Clarke's motorcycle while bracing for his brother's reaction.

"I told you she was a handful. Wait until I tell Madison this one." Craig failed to suppress his laughter. "But got it, I'll reinforce the stranger messaging when I talk to her later."

From there, Kane launched into their father's machinations, from the bad deal with the bank loan to his supposed engagement to Samantha Monroe.

"I'm sorry, Kane. Dad's an ass, but fuck him for not seeing how talented you are. You know that you don't need that building to prove you built it."

"Thanks, man," Kane said, feeling a little lighter. "Brace yourself, though; there's more. That reporter who died in the car accident? His neck was broken before the accident, meaning he was murdered. Trent's team couldn't find any of his work documents except for a backup flash drive. He has a friend at the FBI investigating further."

"Holy shit, that's not good. I say let the sheriff keep investigating, including contacting PCM in any official capacity. The company has nothing to hide." Craig paused before continuing with brotherly seriousness. "And Kane? Keep updating me."

"Will do. I'm sorry I didn't tell you sooner. I just didn't want to burden you with any more bullshit."

"You're my brother. Your burdens are mine."

Thirteen

THE METALLIC WOBBLE OF the measuring tape split the air as Trent called out measurements to Kane. It would give several weeks for the supplies to be delivered, but he planned to return to Mill Creek once they arrived to conduct an inventory and a live walk-through with the general contractor. He wanted to ensure that the contractor understood Trent's desire to preserve some of the charm of his grandfather's home while making necessary upgrades.

No sooner had he written down the measurement than his phone rang. After glancing at the screen, he put the call on speaker.

"Hey, Larry," Kane answered. "I've got you on speaker. What's up, buddy?"

"Remind me of the name of Craig's nanny."

"Annika Bauer. Why?" he asked slowly.

"That's it!" Larry snapped his fingers. "The lead investigator for the firm met with my father yesterday, and as I was walking by, I thought I heard him say Annika's name."

"I'm sure my father requested a thorough background check since she's been employed to work with our family. I wouldn't be surprised if he called the nanny agency to grill them," Kane said.

"I figured as much, but I thought I'd let you know. When you get back, let's get dinner."

"Absolutely, and I appreciate the update." Kane put his phone back in his pocket.

Trent walked up to him. "We're finished. Now get that order placed so I don't miss out on the sale."

"Did anyone ever tell you that you're bossy?"

"You have such a sensitive heart." Trent rolled his eyes. "Do you think your father has a file on me?"

"Probably. Do you want me to call and ask?" Kane asked cheekily.

"That's a hard no."

As his friend started to walk by, Kane grabbed his shoulder. "Hey, how do you feel about me being your neighbor?"

"Why? You thinking of buying the meadow?" Trent looked at him knowingly. "Does this have anything to do with a woman named Annika?"

"She definitely has me thinking about life differently, but I like it here." Kane shrugged. "I could split my time between New York and Mill Creek."

"I love the sound of that, but please buy an appropriate wardrobe. I can't have you running around in designer clothing and tuxedos. You need to learn to wear hiking boots, jeans, and flannels. It's embarrassing, Kane."

Kane raised his eyebrow at Trent. "Stop being a fashionista and take me to the real estate agent's office. I have land to buy."

They made their way into town, parking in front of the Mill Creek Realty Office. A woman in her early forties, dressed in a blue pantsuit, greeted them when they entered. "Hi Sheriff, how can I help you?"

"I'd like to introduce you to my friend, Kane Miller. He's interested in purchasing the meadow area behind my house." Trent's phone started ringing, and he motioned that he was stepping out to answer it.

"Oh, that's a lovely area, but it's pricey," she said, cautiously looking up that parcel of land. "It's 1.25 million, but that would include land, water, and mineral rights."

"I appreciate the information, but that won't be an issue. Can you print me out the specifics along with your contact information?" Kane asked.

The realtor nodded and headed back to her desk to gather the paperwork. She reappeared shortly, handing him a branded folder.

"Excellent, I appreciate your time," he said. "My lawyer will be in contact shortly."

He headed back to Trent's truck, where his friend was still on his phone. Kane slid into the passenger seat and started flipping through the stack of papers, feeling the same surge of excitement he always felt at the start of a new project. Only this time, he would be designing and building his own home.

Trent ended his call and turned to him, his face grim. "That was Noah."

"Do I even want to hear this?" Kane asked.

"After a little bit of digging, Noah found that prior to his political career, Thomas Monroe was a lawyer in Montana. In fact, he was the prosecuting attorney in the rancher's lawsuit against PCM. You told me the case was tossed because the prosecutor didn't have sufficient evidence, but what if I told you that the presiding judge, Judge Jerry Whitehall, over that case also signed off on sealing Monroe's arrest records for gambling and excessive drinking charges?"

Kane frowned. "Whitehall is Penelope's father. Do you think Monroe made some kind of a deal with my dad and Whitehall?"

"Possibly. After that case, he ran and won the governorship, and now he's the Secretary of the Interior."

"And now he's thinking about running for President of the United States. Do you think the reporter was actually investigating the mine or looking for dirt on a potential presidential candidate?"

Trent rested his arm on the top of the steering wheel. "Maybe both?"

"What did Noah find in the thumb drive?" Kane asked, sorting through this new information. Wilcox had to be working to smear Monroe's name. It was the answer that made the most sense.

"He hasn't had a chance to dive into that yet," Trent answered.

He nodded. "Okay, I'll update Craig once Noah finishes reviewing the thumb drive."

Trent turned the key in the ignition and started guiding the truck back to his house when Kane held up his hand to stop him. "I have a favor to ask. Would you be willing to watch Leah for a few hours? I'd like to take Annika on an impromptu date tonight."

Trent's mouth split into a grin. "About damn time, man. Of course, we can find some trouble to get into."

After picking up what Kane needed at the market and getting home, he piled his picnic goodies into a laundry basket, thoughts of Annika sending butterflies fluttering in his stomach. Tonight would be their first time spending time together without the threat of either Leah or Trent interrupting them.

He found that he was addicted to the wonder of Annika Bauer.

Annika had planned to have a quiet evening in until Kane appeared from the kitchen with a bottle of wine and two wine glasses.

Her heart sped up at the sight of him. She noted the subtle scent of sandalwood and cherries from his cologne. He looked relaxed, dressed in his signature dress slacks and a button-down shirt with the top two buttons undone, revealing smooth skin that begged for her touch.

"Come with me," Kane said, putting the wine and glasses in a laundry basket on the counter.

Annika inhaled a quick breath as excitement coursed through her body, her heart beating faster against her chest.

Is this an actual date?

"Uh, I'm not exactly dressed up for whatever you have planned," she replied, her cheeks heating. She looked down at her worn T-shirt and jean shorts while remembering her hair was untamed in a sloppy updo.

"You're gorgeous, Annika. Now, come with me." He picked up the basket, leading her out the door. "I had to improvise, but when we're back in New York, I'll blow your socks off."

"You've already succeeded," she whispered.

Oh my gosh, this man is going to break my heart.

Annika followed him into the backyard, weaving through the aspen trees and across the creek until they stood in the meadow. The sky was streaked purple and orange as the sun started to set. He spread out a blanket and then started unloading the laundry basket. He pulled out a lantern and containers filled with cheese, crackers, and fruit. Once everything was set up, they sat on the blanket together.

Kane had planned a romantic picnic for her. It was perfect. The night had just begun, but it was hands down the best night she had ever had with a man.

She leaned back on the blanket, and he followed, then cupped her face to claim her lips. The kiss was fueled by a passion that caused her body to heat until she felt the beat of her heart at her core.

He broke off the kiss and leaned back to look at her. "You are the best thing that has ever walked into my life, Annika."

When Kane touched her, she lost her damn mind, but when he spoke to her, she felt cherished.

She worked to slow her breathing and gathered her wits. She desperately wanted to know what it would feel like to make love to this man. "Has anyone ever told you that your kisses are dangerous?"

Kane's laughter rumbled from deep in his throat. "No, but I like knowing how much they affect you."

God, if he only knew how much.

Over the next hour or so, they picnicked, shared stories, and laughed at their differences. Her body hummed from being so close to him. While she knew without a doubt that his intentions were pure, her mother's words still echoed in her head.

"I really like you, but I also don't want to blur the lines any more than this," she said, craning her neck upwards to see his face. "I'm here to watch Leah, and she and your brother don't deserve less from me."

"Annika, the pace is yours to set, and I'll always respect it. I'm not going anywhere because being by your side is my favorite place to be."

She realized that she had more room in her heart for happiness than fear and distrust. Somewhere along the way, she'd fallen hard for Kane. Maybe it was his boyish charm when trying something new, or his big heart and loyalty to those who mattered to him. Although he was a billionaire, he didn't worship money as much as his own personal worth.

"Thanks, Kane, for tonight. It's one night I'll never forget." After a moment, she whispered, "This piece of land is beautiful."

Kane nuzzled her head. "It is a special place."

Stars dotted the sky while the soft sounds of the creek flowed behind them. They continued to enjoy each other's company for a while, discussing favorite movies and Broadway shows before settling into the silence of just being together.

Deciding that it was time to head home, they made quick work of repacking the basket before indulging in a lingering kiss. Hand in hand, they followed the same path and entered Trent's home through the back door. The house was quiet.

"Tonight was special," Annika said, then lifted on her tiptoes to press another soft kiss to his lips. She headed back to her bedroom. She settled into bed, her whole body vibrating with desire and happiness. It had been so long since she felt hopeful about what was to come.

Her body started to drift into a deep rest when she heard a knock at her door, Kane's deep voice following.

"Annika, sweetheart. Wake up." Kane opened the door and stood at the threshold. "There's a phone call for you. It's the nanny agency; they called me when they were unable to reach you."

Annika's eyes snapped open. She sat upright and grabbed her phone off the nightstand. "Shoot, I forgot to charge my phone."

She got up and walked out toward the family room with Kane right on her heels. Annika's heart seized, and her stomach plummeted when she reached for the phone.

Oh God, please let my parents be okay.

"This is Annika," she answered.

"I'm sorry to call at such a late hour, but your apartment has been broken into," Nancy started, her voice laced with concern. "Your building manager called NYPD, and when they couldn't reach you, they called us. The police had also mentioned that your car was damaged a week ago. Is that right?"

"Yes, unfortunately. Did they provide a contact person?"

"They did. Officer Rolo, the same officer who's handling your vehicle. Are you okay?" Nancy asked.

"I'll be fine. I'll give Officer Rolo a call." Annika replied, sucking down a deep breath. "Thanks, Nancy."

When she ended the call, she felt two sets of eyes drilling holes into her head. The couch cushions dipped under Kane's weight. When his arm wrapped around her, she fought to keep her tears from falling, fought the urge to give in to the misery consuming her.

Trent backed out of the room, leaving them alone.

"What happened, sweetheart?" he asked.

"I chose a horrible building to live in. Now, my apartment has been broken into, and I have to call the police back," she said, her lip quivering.

"Say the word, Annika, and I'll contact them for you. Whatever you need, it's yours," Kane reassured her.

The last bit of her energy faded. She wanted this cycle to end...wanted to just live her life without having to contact the police. She rested her head on his shoulder and twined her fingers through his, enjoying his warmth and the connection to someone who grounded her.

"I would really appreciate it if the universe left me alone for a while," Annika said, squeezing his hand. "But instead, I need to make this call. I'll put it on speaker."

Kane dialed the number and held it between them until the call had been transferred to Officer Rolo.

The officer picked up quickly. "Miss Bauer, I'm sorry that we keep meeting under these circumstances. The door to your apartment was kicked open, and the inside was ransacked. My team has collected evidence, but we will need you to conduct a walk-through to determine whether anything specific was taken. When will you be back in town?"

"We're scheduled to return on Saturday," Annika answered.

"Officer, this is Kane Miller. We spoke the other day. I can have us back later today and then we can meet on Thursday morning. Does that work?"

Annika turned to Kane and mouthed, "You're on vacation."

When Kane's hand reached out to cup her cheek, his gaze shone with sincerity. She leaned into his touch, wanting to absorb every ounce of his warmth.

"Yes. Time is critical in these types of investigations. Let's plan to meet outside of Ms. Bauer's building on Thursday, say eleven a.m."

"Will do," Kane responded.

After they hung up, Annika sat back against the sofa, tossing her head against the cushion to stare at the ceiling. "I don't want you to sacrifice your vacation for my crappy life."

Kane twisted to see her face. "I'm not. It's my choice."

"Thanks. I appreciate not having to do this alone." Annika glanced down at his phone. "It's almost five. Let me grab my wallet so I can book a flight. What time do you think you and Leah will be leaving?"

Kane's eyebrows bunched up. "Why? You're coming with us. I'll charter a plane, so we don't have to wait for the jet to fly here from New York. It'll be easier."

Annika framed his face with her hands. "That's my point. You're having to pay money to get me back to New York. Maybe I should just go, but Leah—"

Kane grabbed her wrists. "Sweetheart, I chose to support you not because you aren't strong enough, but because you're important to me. So, please put me out of my misery and let me help."

Annika couldn't stop the smile that curved the corners of her mouth. "Fine."

Kane smiled back. "If we leave by eleven, we should be in New York by dinner. Will you let Leah know we are flying home? I'll go talk to Trent."

In a whirl of activity, Annika showered and packed before focusing on Leah. Once everything was ready, she joined Kane and Trent in the kitchen. The car and driver showed up minutes later to take them to the airport. It was barely ten in the morning, and she was already exhausted.

Trent carried Leah out front, who cried in his arms. "I love you."

"I love you too, kiddo," Trent said, patting her back. "Promise me next time you come back to visit that you'll bring your dad."

"Oh, that would be fun," Leah said, her tears pausing for a moment. Once on the ground, she ran over to Kane, who was speaking to the driver.

Annika took that opportunity to hug Trent. "Thank you for everything."

"Anytime, Annika. Take care of that overdressed man over there."

"I heard that, buddy," Kane scowled. He opened the door for Leah, who climbed into the backseat of the big black SUV. "This suit is a custom beauty from Italy."

And it fits him like a glove, she thought to herself.

Trent split the distance with Kane before embracing him in a quick hug. "I appreciate the disruption you brought to my home. All of this chaos reminded me that there is still good in life."

"There is. I'll always be here for you." Kane grabbed Trent's shoulder. "I'll be back when the renovation starts to get things started off right."

"I'll hold you to that. I'll call you when I get Noah's update on the flash drive."

Fourteen

ANNIKA'S NERVES POUNDED LIKE little monsters looking to escape. She had no desire to see her studio. Her safe place had been violated again, and she did not have the energy to work through her feelings about it. Having lived through this once, she was not looking forward to seeing yellow police tape, discarded gloves, and whatever damage the intruder had done.

She slid her gaze toward Kane, who chatted with the valet outside his building. Last night, it was illuminated by lights, but in the daylight, it was beautiful. His father was an idiot for not seeing his talent in every aspect of this building, down to the neutral palette, the sleek cabinetry, and the marble finishes. Kane should be proud of what he created.

"This is impressive, Kane. I love it," she said, gesturing at the building. If Annika had not been watching him, she would have missed the quick flash of sadness that shot across his face. It gutted her to know how much Kane's father had hurt him. Here she was, worried about herself, while Kane was experiencing the worst kind of betrayal at the hands of his own father.

She wrapped her arms around him and squeezed. "Your dad can never take this away. This building *you* designed and built will always be yours."

He held her in his embrace until she heard a vehicle approaching. An older man exited the driver's side and walked around to greet Kane.

Different nervous monsters twisted in her stomach. She was about to meet the man that Kane revered.

"You should have called me. I would have been happy to pick you all up last night," Albert said to Kane. "Thank you for the flowers, though. Linda loved the arrangement."

"No way, it was your anniversary. And Linda deserves nothing less," Kane said.

"Well, I agree with you there," Albert said. Then he walked over to Annika, his hand extended. "I'm Albert Scott. It's nice to meet you, Annika."

A burst of emotion propelled her forward, ignoring his hand to hug him instead. "The pleasure is all mine. Kane has told me so much about you and your wife."

"This kid is all heart," Albert said, patting Kane on the chest. "Now, where's Leah? I was looking forward to a game of I Spy."

Kane laughed, opening the door for Annika. "She's going to the Natural History Museum today with another nanny."

Once they were all inside, Albert drove forward, merging into traffic. "So, to Annika's apartment?"

"Yes," Kane answered before grabbing her hand to kiss the back of it.

It occurred to her that if she had not endured all that she had, she would have never met Kane. Could this be her silver lining? That thought warmed her insides.

As they drove, Kane pointed out specific buildings or architectural styles, such as art deco, gothic, and beaux arts. She loved experiencing the city through his eyes. It felt like an intimate way to look directly into his soul.

The vehicle eventually pulled up to the curb in front of her building. When she glanced out the window, she saw Officer Rolo standing next to a woman wearing a gray suit and a badge hanging around her neck. Her stomach tightened as Kane and she exited the vehicle.

"Hello, Ms. Bauer, Mr. Miller," Officer Rolo said. He motioned to the woman next to him. "This is Detective Ruso."

"I appreciate you coming home early to deal with all of this," the detective said, shaking their hands before handing them her business cards. "I've been investigating a string of parking garage burglaries. My captain added your apartment to my assignment to see if this was an escalation."

"Were no other units in her building broken into? Just Annika's?" Kane looked puzzled.

Ruso nodded. "If you're ready, let's head upstairs."

Annika inhaled, hoping the rush of oxygen would quell the nerves that had flared again. The slow march to her front door seemed endless. When they reached her splintered front door, she paused, noticing the giant piece of plywood to the right of it.

"Is that piece of plywood to close off her front doorway until it's fixed?" Kane asked.

"Yes, Officer Rolo will stay with the unit until the manager comes up to secure it," the detective replied dispassionately. "Okay, Ms. Bauer, take your time and tell us if you notice anything unusual or missing. It's a mess in there."

It was all she could do not to snap. *No shit*. But while the detective was doing her job with zero empathy, it wasn't as if she knew Annika's past. Once inside her apartment, Annika's gaze darted around the space. This was not even close to what she had experienced last time.

Everything was trashed. Her pillows were slashed. Her clothing was in tatters. Everything that could be smashed had been shattered.

"How had this happened without anyone hearing?" Kane asked.

Annika went over to where her dresser had been overturned. She squatted, moving items on the floor, looking for the box she kept in the top drawer. It contained a small pouch of fine jewelry, her passport, and both sets of car keys. A tendril of dread crawled down her spine.

"I can't find it," she moaned, her movements becoming more frantic.

Kane bent down next to her and placed his hand on her back. "What are we looking for?"

"A thin box, it has—"

Kane handed her a flattened box. "Is this it?"

"Yes," She took it, removing the lid to reveal the contents. She opened the felt pouch and pulled a ring free. "It was my mother's engagement ring. My dad had upgraded her ring for their thirtieth anniversary, so she gave this to me when I graduated from UCLA."

"It's beautiful," Kane said.

Her mind flashed with an image of Kane on bended knee, giving her a ring. Her body sparkled as the future of what could be whirled across her mind. This repugnant situation surrounding her faded because what mattered the most sat next to her.

Annika slid the ring onto her finger, then hugged her hand to her chest. "It's strange. Nothing seems to have been taken. Do you think they were interrupted?"

The detective entered. "Do you see anything missing?"

"No, it looks like everything was just destroyed."

Ruso pulled her notepad out and jotted down a note. "Do you know of anyone who would wish you harm or had an altercation with you recently?"

Annika shook her head. "No, not anyone here."

"Other places?" Ruso did not look up from her notes.

Annika swallowed. "I had a stalker in Los Angeles, but he's behind bars."

The detective stopped taking notes and looked up at her. Her lips flattened. "What's his name?"

Annika provided Folley's name and reached for Kane's hand. Just knowing he stood by her side gave her the strength to endure the police process she had done too many times.

Ruso peered at Annika. "A neighbor described a slender man about five feet, ten inches tall, fleeing near your apartment, but they didn't see his face. Does that description match anyone you know?"

"No. I'm still new to the city," Annika answered, shaking her head.

"Okay. On my way out, I'll give the building manager the green light to begin repairs." The detective shifted her gaze between Annika and Kane. "I'll be in contact if anything else comes up. If you need me, you have my number."

Kane kept his hand at the small of her back, guiding her from the building until they reached the car. Albert held the back car door open for her. Once the door closed, encased in her protective cocoon, Annika let out a long sigh. She did not want to live there again. She would always be reminded of what happened.

"You're thinking entirely too hard over there," Kane noted from beside her. He pressed a button and a divider slid up between Albert and them.

A groan slipped from her lips as he slid his hand under her hair to lightly massage her neck. The tension in her neck started to ebb. "I'm adding filing a claim with my insurance company and finding a new place to live to my to-do list. I wonder if I can get my security deposit back?"

"You can stay with me at my place for as long as you'd like so that you don't have to rush finding something," Kane replied.

He pulled her closer, lowering his mouth to kiss her. The kiss was tender, passionate, and emotional. He coaxed her mind and body into a wonder-filled dimension. The sorrow from the moments before started to ebb.

"I want to take you home," he whispered, wrapping his hand in her hair. His lips covered her own once more. "We'll have my place to ourselves until Leah comes home."

Annika's pulse quickened at the mere thought of finally getting to make love with Kane. Deep down, she knew they belonged together, like two puzzle pieces clicking together to complete an image.

At his building, Kane's sense of urgency as he ushered her into the elevator exhilarated her. His heavy gaze never left hers as they ascended to his floor. His intense stare made her feel like she was his prey.

A wicked sense of power and lust slammed into her body once they entered his apartment. She walked onto his terrace, teasing him as she knew what was to come. She did not have to turn around to know he was following her. The heat from his body penetrated her back as he stood against her.

"I love how the Hudson sparkles," she said, leaning her head back against his chest. His erection pressed firmly against her bottom.

He turned her around and rubbed his thumb across her bottom lip. "The best view is the one standing before me."

Her heart melted. She pressed close to him, taking up every molecule of space until they were one unit. Her nipples hardened, and her body hummed as every nerve ending came alive, wanting, needing, craving this man's touch. She had fantasized about this moment so often, and there was no way she was stopping it now.

"I want you, Kane," she murmured. She ran her hands up his chest, loving how she could feel his muscles tighten under her fingertips. Then, she slid her hand downward, watching his eyes dilate the further down she went. She cupped his erection through his pants, moving her hand back and forth over his hardened length.

A guttural moan tore from his lips. He threaded his fingers through her hair and tilted her head to his liking. When her mouth opened for him, his tongue invaded her, touching and stroking every part of her before he deepened the kiss. If a declaration could be made by a kiss, he'd just marked her for life.

He released her mouth long enough to pull her shirt up and over her head. Tiny goose bumps covered her warm skin. Her bra followed, falling from her body. Kane cupped her breasts, squeezing them together gently before rolling her nipples between his thumbs and forefingers. The sensation, a mixture of pain and pleasure, sent a wave of moisture to her core. His continual torment made her nipples harden even more.

"Sweetheart, is this what you want? For me to make love to you?"

"Yes, Kane," Annika murmured. She ran her hands back up his chest, grabbing each side of his shirt and pulling hard, buttons clattering across the travertine stones. She needed to feel his skin against hers.

He slid his hands down her body until he cupped her ass. He then lifted her, causing her to wrap her legs around him, and carried her into the living room. When he set her down on the couch, she peeled back the material of his shirt to reveal a sculpted chest.

She loved his body—hard, chiseled, and entirely hers. His heat sizzled against her palms as she ran her fingertips over his pecs and along the rippling muscles of his stomach. Fueled by passion, she ripped the remnants of his shirts from his pants until his shirt hit the floor.

Her hand dipped lower, meeting his hands, fumbling with zippers and more buttons.

"Still too many clothes," she said breathlessly.

"Take them off," he demanded as he stepped back to pull his pants free from his body.

She had never wanted or needed someone as badly as she did Kane. She fumbled briefly with her own pants before sliding them down her legs, forgetting about the ugly scars that she usually tried to hide. She reached out and grasped the waistband of his boxer briefs, yanking them down muscular legs. His erection sprang free, jutting from a neatly trimmed patch of dark hair. Licking her bottom lip, she stared at his length before sinking down to her knees.

It was time to claim what she wanted. There was no preamble, only a deep sense of belonging. She took him into her mouth, the subtle scent of sandalwood mingling with an earthy taste that was all Kane. A sigh of pleasure escaped her throat before she gripped his shaft and began to stroke.

A deep groan of satisfaction rumbled from Kane. "As much as I love your mouth on me, I need to be inside of you."

In one fluid move, he pulled from her mouth. He bent down to retrieve a foil packet from his discarded wallet and sheathed his cock.

"You ready, sweetheart?"

"Yes," she murmured, watching him stroke his cock.

He tore her panties from her body and pulled her up from the couch. He slid his fingers between her slick folds, tormenting her bundle of nerves, as he pressed her back against the wall. Instinctively, she wrapped her legs around his waist, prompting him to move his hands upward to grip the globes of her ass. Then, he angled her body so he could align his cock to her entrance. Slowly, he entered her, stretching her muscles to accommodate his girth.

He worked his length back and forth, gaining a few inches until he sank deep. His grip on her tightened as she felt him withdraw and surge inside her. He began to thrust deeper and harder. His rhythm was steady but thorough as he increased his tempo. Capable, strong hands held her as her body hummed with delight.

Small whimpers of pleasure rumbled from her throat as she clamped down on his cock. She loved how he filled and took control of her body. A delicious ache intensified in her core, driving higher with each movement as her climax intensified.

Sweat dampened his flesh. “You are incredible. I’m not going to last.”

She would take this moment and treasure it forever. As his strokes became more frenzied, she found herself going over the edge, pleasure rushing through her body. Her cries of passion were swallowed by his mouth as he kissed her passionately.

He pounded deep until he paused and growled her name.

The only sound that filled the condominium was their ragged breaths.

She felt content being in his arms as they enjoyed the aftermath of the best sex she had ever had. When did she become this wanton woman? She didn't know and didn't care. With Kane, everything was perfect.

Lifting her head to look at his face, she said, “This was holy moly amazing, but to be sure it wasn't a fluke, we’ll need to do it again. You know...for comparison’s sake.”

“Is that so? And here I thought I needed to offer myself to you again so that you could finish what your wicked mouth started earlier,” he teased before nipping her bottom lip.

He adjusted his grip on her before turning away from the wall with her in his arms. As he padded down the hallway toward his bedroom, the slight change in position caused her to grind down against him, eliciting a growl to escape his lips. His body was primed and ready to go again.

"Ready for round two?" he asked, his voice low and husky. "This time will be slow and deliberate because I want to enjoy every inch of your beautiful body."

He put her down on his bed before heading to his bathroom to dispose of the condom. She watched the muscles in his ass flex and move with every step. Who was she to say no to a hot man who wanted to possess her body while making her wildest dreams come true?

But could she make *his* dreams come true?

Fifteen

THE SUN FILTERED THROUGH the shutters in Kane's bedroom. He turned to find one half of his bed empty.

Since Leah was still visiting, Annika slept in the guest room. As much as he admired Annika's principles, a selfish part of him wanted her lying next to him, where she belonged. Kane's chest swelled as he could no longer deny that she was his perfect match in so many ways. This amazing woman was open, honest, and funny. She gave all of herself to those around her. She was so full of love and life. Her innocent enthusiasm made him smile.

His body was sated and happy after making love to Annika yesterday afternoon. After he showered, shaved, and dressed, he walked over to his nightstand and opened the drawer to retrieve the fifty-dollar bill, her bra, and the shirt he had put there last night when he remembered they had started their tryst outside.

He walked down the hallway, picking up the subtle scent of lavender and vanilla. Knocking on her door, he waited until a bright smile, and beautiful brown eyes greeted him.

He entered and tugged her into a hug. "I missed you last night."

"I missed you too. What's up?"

He raised a curious eyebrow. "I picked up your clothing from the deck last night and found this fifty-dollar bill under your bra. Is that a tip for me?"

She groaned inwardly and then giggled. "It was in my bra."

"Your bra?" he asked, his curiosity deepening.

She took the fifty out of his hand. "My father gave it to me when I moved here to make sure I'd always have taxi fare in case my purse is stolen. He told me to put it somewhere safe, and so, since I was wearing sandals, my bra seemed like the next best place."

Kane threw his head back and laughed. "I do like adventures, sweetheart. I'll have to find where you put it every time I undress you."

He watched as her mouth popped open to respond. Instead, she snapped him with her bra. He shook his head, retreating from her room and towards the kitchen. His cheeks burned from the size of his smile.

Oh yes, life with Annika will never be dull.

Kane's cell phone rang, and after he glanced at the screen, he headed to the deck instead. He leaned against the railing. The faint sounds of traffic drifted upward.

"I knew you were going to miss my smiling face," Kane said.

"Nah, you were a pain in the ass, but Annika and Leah were a good distraction," Trent answered. "How did yesterday go?"

"Annika handled it, but her apartment was trashed. What burglar takes the risk to break and not take anything? I know you confirmed that her stalker is still in prison, but it seemed personal."

"Sorry, man. I'm here if you need anything," Trent offered. "Noah did his magic with the data on the thumb drive, and the rabbit hole has expanded significantly. It appears that Wilcox was focused on PCM. There was information about the Warwick Mine, Alaska, and Montana."

"Did he uncover new evidence? Or was he trying to drive the public's negative perception of PCM?"

"In this case, the public would be right to be leery. Someone was trying to cover up the damage. Wilcox found a source who said her father signed an NDA with a representative from the law firm Behr & Goldstein and was paid a monthly stipend through the end of Monroe's gubernatorial term. It seems he had enough evidence and motive to expose PCM. That provides us with a likely motive for his murder."

"If my father has all this on Monroe, why is he forcing the marriage?"

A car horn blared in the background. "My best guess is that Monroe hasn't been as influential or as loyal as your father would have liked. Maybe having you marry his daughter is another way to keep him in line. The stakes certainly seem high enough."

Kane watched the boats cutting through the waters. "Craig is not going to like any of this when he hears about it, but he won't betray Noah. So, what's the Sheriff's Office's official stance?"

"The media have been waiting on the autopsy results, so I'll provide them with an update at the end of the week that, while Wilcox's death has been ruled a homicide, the investigation is ongoing. That alone will elevate the story," Trent answered.

"I'll only update Craig," Kane said. "Hey, I've got to go. My father is calling, but I'll talk to you later."

He frowned; he couldn't remember the last time his father called from his private number. Still irritated by the latest update from Trent, he answered the phone with no warmth in his tone.

"As your father, I'm willing to give you a final chance to right your wrong. We can stop all further action if you marry Samantha within the next two weeks."

"Ah, an exchange of two lives for my building. Is that what you mean?"

"You are insufferable, Kane Patrick Miller. You damn well know actions have consequences. This olive branch is simply a way to salvage your mistake and prevent others from getting hurt."

"As I said, I'm finished. I'm not subjecting Samantha or myself to this obscene demand. Figure out your own situation."

There was a long pause on his father's end. "It's not in your best interest to go against me. Are you so selfish that you're willing to risk your beloved brother being removed from my succession plan, losing everything he's built for PMC?"

"You're delusional," Kane scoffed. "*You're* willing to destroy your company, which you put above all else in our entire lives, if I don't fall in line? Maybe it's time for a change in leadership, because you're not making sound judgments."

"Careful, son. All you have to do is marry Samantha by the end of this month, and everything stops." The line ended.

Kane inhaled sharply. *Fucking asshole!*

His chest tightened with dread. He never imagined his father would remove Craig from the company, but now he wasn't so sure. Had he destroyed everything his brother had worked his life to achieve?

"Kane, are you okay?" Annika asked from behind him.

No, he wasn't okay. If he turned to look at her, he might crumble. He kept staring at the currents. "I'm in the middle of a situation. I'll be in later."

When he heard the sliding door close, he lowered his head and closed his eyes. A list of phone calls popped into his head: Trent, Samantha...Craig. With each ring of the phone as he waited for Craig to answer, his chest continued to constrict.

"Were your ears burning?" Craig asked.

"No, but you sound like you're flying," Kane said.

"Surprise! London is a wrap, so Madison and I are headed back to New York," Craig announced excitedly. "Plus, I miss Leah. It's far too quiet without her. I'll be by to pick her up tomorrow."

"That's great. She'll be happy to see you." He walked over to a chair and sat down. "I've got some bad news. Noah cracked open the flash drive and my most recent conversation with Dad went sideways fast. Which update do you want first?"

"Okay. Start with Noah's findings."

Kane told him everything that Trent had shared from Noah's deep dive. "Trent is going to announce that the reporter's accident is a homicide. I haven't said a word to Dad, but you should know since it will be common notice soon enough."

"Interesting coincidence that Penelope's father is involved in this," Craig murmured.

"Yeah, I'm still not sure what role he played in this other than sealing Monroe's records, but our father found Monroe's vulnerability and is exploiting it. Regardless, the optics don't look great for anyone between the NDAs, possible bribes, and the fact that PCM was the target of the lawsuit."

"Sure, but it will all come down to whether it can be proved that they acted illegally or immorally. I would bet my job that Walter Behr has ensured Dad has plausible deniability since he handles all his legal affairs," Craig pointed out. "I'll follow the money and figure out which account the stipends were coming from and where they were going."

"That might be a problem." Kane struggled to swallow. "Speaking of dear old Dad, I thought he was trying to intimidate me into marrying Samantha, but he threatened to terminate and remove you from his succession planning if I don't follow through."

"That's preposterous," Craig spat out. "All he has ever cared about is PCM's legacy. He's not going to turn it over to an outsider. Stand your ground and let him rage. He'll figure out another way to get what he wants with Monroe."

"I don't know, Craig. You could lose everything because of me. He seems desperate to make this happen." Kane was becoming increasingly uneasy the longer they had this conversation. The silence over the line extended a bit too long for comfort. "Craig? Did you hear me?"

"It just occurred to me that Penelope died from a broken neck," he answered quietly. "We'll talk more tomorrow. I need some time to process all of this."

Kane's head spun as he hung up. He hadn't realized that had been Penelope's cause of death from the accident. Could she have been murdered, too, for threatening their father?

Kane sent Trent a quick message: *Craig told me that Penelope also died from a broken neck when she had her car accident. Have Noah investigate further.*

He stared at the three dots on his screen until Trent's response came back.

Will do.

A sickening thought occurred to him. His father could be brutal, but an injured animal was unpredictable. He did not know how far this father would go. He needed to warn Samantha to get as far away from their fathers' reach, but now he needed to protect Annika, too.

"Hey Samantha, how are you doing?"

"Not the best," she answered. "I signed the documents, but Dad's not happy. He just heard that you haven't signed them yet."

"Do you know why your father is backing this marriage? Do you think this has to do with him becoming president?"

"Not sure. He's been ranting about how he's tired of being controlled, how everyone wants time on his calendar, or some promise he'll fulfill once he's in office." She let out a frustrated sigh. "I know that Bruce and my dad have a history. I remember him visiting us for years when we lived in Montana. Maybe your father is pushing some agenda on him."

A derisive half-laugh escaped Kane's mouth. "Something is going on. Don't worry, though. My dad can try to strongarm me, but I'm not signing those documents."

"This is getting out of control," Samantha said.

"I agree. Listen, I don't want you to get caught in the middle of whatever is happening between those two. Don't tell anyone where you're going, but take an extended vacation with your boyfriend. Book the tickets and send me the bill. Do it today."

"Really?" she asked brightly.

"I'm serious. Get it arranged and get gone. The faster the better." Kane's voice softened. "Samantha? Make it the trip of a lifetime."

He hung up, then stood and rubbed at his head, hoping the oncoming headache would subside. When he walked back inside his apartment, he saw Leah and Annika coloring on the coffee table.

"Uncle Kane, you missed breakfast," Leah said.

"I'm sorry. Sometimes, business can't wait," Kane responded. He noticed that Annika was watching him. He was not ready to share everything with her yet. He needed time to think.

"I do have some good news, Leah." He tried to force a little happiness into his flat mood.

"What?" she asked, her eyes going wide.

"Your daddy and Madison will be home tomorrow morning." As his niece celebrated, dancing around the apartment, he looked at Annika. "I need to do some work. Will you help Leah get packed?"

Without another word, he made his way down the hallway. As he approached his office door, he felt Annika's hand on his elbow.

"What's happening, Kane? I know something is wrong."

He looked right into her eyes. "Please get Leah ready. I don't want to be pestered."

"I'm sorry, that's not my intention. Let me know if you need anything," she said quietly.

"I need you to do your job. That's it." He regretted his words the second they left his mouth, watching her eyes flash with hurt. "It's just... Leave me be, Annika."

He turned away, closing the door behind him. He'd explain it to her later. Right now, he needed to figure out how to keep his decision from costing Craig everything.

Sixteen

ANNIKA DID NOT SEE Kane the rest of last night.

She understood that he was upset, but he had never been so cold and rude to her. Her hurt fed a small niggle of doubt that had her questioning if they were together anymore. She did not want to believe that, but when she saw his note on the kitchen counter in the morning, she felt no relief.

Please tell Leah I love her. I'm off to a meeting—K

The doorbell chimed. Leah almost ran into the door in her haste to open it. "Daddy! I missed you."

"Ladybug, I missed you more." Craig, looking so similar to Kane, twirled her around in his arms. "It's nice to finally meet you in person, Annika. Madison wanted to be here, but she isn't feeling well."

Annika smiled. "You're raising an impressive young lady."

"Where is my brother hiding?" Craig asked, looking around.

"He had an early meeting," she answered tightly. "However, Leah, he did say that he loves you and had so much fun with you."

Leah turned around in her father's arms. "I had fun too, Daddy. Can we have a tea party when we get home?"

Craig winked at Annika. "Of course, Ladybug. Let's get your stuff."

While Leah fetched her belongings, he handed Annika an envelope. "Thank you for everything. You are wonderful. I have left you a glowing review with the agency."

"Oh, thank you, but Leah made it pretty easy," she said, accepting the envelope, which was heavier than she expected.

She closed and locked the door behind them once they left. Her jaw nearly dropped when she opened the envelope and saw a stack of one-hundred-dollar bills secured with a band labeled *five thousand dollars*. Tucked into the band was a handwritten note.

Annika, please accept this token as my appreciation for going above and beyond. You not only cared for my baby girl, but you also made a difference in her life. Sincerely, Craig M. Miller

Tears fell down her cheeks. She already missed Leah's presence, knowing her assignment was over. She had no clue where she stood with Kane, knowing he did not want to see her. How could her life have crumbled into a state of despair in the blink of an eye? The agony of starting over hit her right in the face.

In her pocket, her phone vibrated with an incoming text: "*Your unit is ready." The door and frame have been repaired. Please stop by the office to pick up your new keys.* She had to find a new place to live. She had no desire to stay in that apartment any longer than it took to clean it and pack up anything that may have survived.

Annika opened the sliding glass door, craving fresh air. The early morning rays of light kissed the Hudson River in the distance. She looked down at people going about their weekend activities. She mentally compiled her checklist of what she had to accomplish today.

Her first stop had to be the nanny agency to turn in her final report.

Then she needed to find a hotel to stay for a few nights until she found a new place to live. Maybe, if she were lucky, she could get her security deposit back, given the situation.

And she needed to replace her furniture and clothing, but she could do so in time.

Annika jumped into the shower and let the hot spray sluice down her body. After showering, she dried off, slathered on her favorite lotion, and blow-dried and styled her hair. For extra pep, she did not feel, she even applied a light layer of makeup.

She was about to order a taxi to leave when she heard the doorbell ring again. She hesitated briefly. Should she answer or ignore the door?

When she eventually opened it, she saw an older woman impeccably dressed in a designer suit tailored to fit her petite frame. Her honey blonde hair and makeup were flawless. The most beautiful pair of hazel eyes stared back at her. Now she knew from whom Kane got his eyes.

"You must be Annika."

Annika felt self-conscious about the jean shorts and T-shirt she had decided to wear today. Her insides quivered like Jell-O at his mother's presence. How did Caroline Miller even know she was here?

"Hi. Please come in." She stepped back and motioned for Caroline to enter.

The matriarch of the family glided past her, heading down the hallway toward the living room. The only sound that trailed her was the clicking of her heels against the hard floor. She gracefully took a seat on the edge of the sofa and patted the seat cushion next to her. "Where is my son?"

"Uh, Kane isn't home," Annika said, feeling wrong for sharing that bit of information as she trailed her down the hallway. "He said he has a meeting."

"I'm assuming Craig came by to pick up Leah?"

Annika did not know how she had known all this information, but she also did not know what Kane might have shared with his mother during their silent break last night. "Yes. They left about an hour ago."

"Perfect. I'd rather speak to you, anyway. Kane can be rather obstinate when it suits him." Caroline sat perfectly straight, her ankles crossed, her slim, shapely legs pressed together, leaning slightly to the right. Even her hands were clasped in her lap. It reminded her of how the Queen of England sat.

Annika hesitated for a moment before she took a seat, regretting her decision to open the front door. Her mind whirled with all the reasons as to why his mother wanted to speak to her. The warning bells in her head told her that this was not a purely social call.

"If I remember correctly, you're a UCLA graduate with a degree in psychology," Caroline said. "Helping others is a noble profession, a similarity we share. I see why my son is smitten with you."

She was caught off guard. Based on the way Kane had spoken about his mother, she had not expected him to share any personal details about her life with her. Her stomach settled a little and she chastised herself for assuming the worst about Caroline.

"Yes, he mentioned that you take great pride in your philanthropic work. It's nice to give back to your community." Annika cleared her throat.

Caroline nodded. "In my social circle, it's important to balance your time between various types of events and fundraising. Although, image is everything. In fact, that's why I'm here today."

Annika's stomach tightened again. She forced a smile on her face, bracing herself for whatever brutal honesty would follow.

"In our family, we protect our image and interests at all costs. Last night, Kane chose not to honor an obligation. Now, because of his selfishness, he is about to learn a difficult lesson that will also have consequences for his brother. It seems that Bruce is making changes to his executive team at PCM."

The blood drained from Annika's face as she listened to Caroline. He was being punished for living his life on his own terms, and it broke her heart.

"Why?" Annika's voice was strangled as she forced the words past the knot in her throat.

"Kane has expectations and responsibilities to his family. His marriage to Samantha must happen. Telling his father no last night was a mistake. My goal today is to salvage the situation and to help him reverse his decision."

Annika didn't know what to say as her chest constricted.

Caroline continued. "Bruce is committed to safeguarding his family, but I am worried that he has no limits in pursuing his goal. You need to understand what's at stake."

Annika sat quietly, scared by the implied threat.

"Your presence in our lives has caused irreparable damage, but if you leave now the plans we put into motion will stop." Kane's mother stood, swiping imaginary wrinkles from her skirt. "Think about what I said, Annika. I appreciate your time."

The sound of Caroline's high heels faded until the thud of the front door signaled her departure.

Kane had chosen Annika, which meant she would take the decision out of his hands.

Tears streamed down her face. She never told Kane that she loved him, and she never would. She went to the kitchen and wrote the hardest note of her life.

Kane, what we had together was fun, but it's time to move on. Focus on your family and life, and let's make this a clean break. ~Annika

More tears stung her eyes as she glanced at the clock. The last thing she wanted was to be here when Kane got home, or her conviction would crumble like stale bread. She ordered her taxi, gathered her bags, and headed downstairs to the curb.

She chose a hotel close to her apartment, so she could work through the mess. When she stopped by her place to meet with the manager, she was disappointed that he would not return her security deposit, saying that that was life.

She knew damn well how life could throw a person curveballs. Exhaustion had consumed her body. She forced her feet to carry her away from Kane, numb to everything around her. Her chest ached, like her heart had a fifty-pound weight attached to it.

Her heart broke for Kane. She could not imagine how rotten and betrayed he must feel again, knowing it was his own father who had done it. She had cost him everything because he had chosen her, and that knowledge made her stomach flop. There was no choice but to leave, but physically doing it gutted her. Unconditional love was greater than a person.

On autopilot, she went through the motions of checking in at the front desk, paying with the cash Craig had given her. After the clerk showed her how to get to her room, she entered the elevator with her key card in hand.

"What floor, miss?" A man asked as he entered behind her, his luggage filling the remaining space.

"Sixteen," she replied somberly.

When the elevator dinged on her floor, she exited the car. The hallway featured a highly patterned carpet designed to conceal signs of wear and tear. The walls were painted a neutral color and adorned with framed pictures of places around the city. The air smelled of furniture polish and room freshener, both stale and overpowering.

When she found her room, she slid the key card into the automated lock until the reader flashed a green light. She opened the door, and a partial view of the city greeted her. The city's lights began to twinkle as darkness took over from the setting sun.

She would treasure the time they had spent together, but sometimes destiny had a mind of its own. God, she had to stop as another pang of regret ripped through her chest. The sharp melodic sound of her phone broke into the silence. She glanced at her screen, curious when she saw her lawyer in Los Angeles calling so late.

"Hi," Annika greeted him. "Ah, let me guess, you picked up my stuff from the detective?"

"Yes, but that's not why I'm calling." He paused. "I received a call that Mike Folley secured a new high-powered law firm that sought to reduce his sentence to time served or move him to house arrest for the remainder of his sentence."

The room spun as Annika moved to the bed to sit. "Are you kidding me?"

"I'd never joke about something like this, Annika."

"How is that even possible? He tried to kill me."

Her lawyer exhaled before speaking. "Overcrowding is an opportunity for lawyers to advocate for their clients, mostly first-time offenders, who have been model prisoners. An attorney with a good reputation from a well-respected firm will hold clout. Folley's new legal team did their research. They argued that he was never tied to any of the previous attacks against you and that it was a first-time offense for reckless driving with bodily injury."

Annika closed her eyes, trying not to yell. "That bastard doesn't deserve anything. He should remain in jail. He. Tried. To. Kill. Me."

"I know, and I'm sorry. The creep should remain in jail, but the judge approved his house arrest. Once the paperwork is signed, Folley will be released into home custody with an ankle monitor and check-in schedule."

"That's ridiculous." Annika's voice wobbled from her tears. "Why even bother going through pressing charges?"

"Because now that he's gone to prison, he has a record. His time in prison wasn't going to be forever. He's still incarcerated now, even if he isn't behind bars. They will monitor him." Her attorney sighed. "Just keep in mind that Mike Folley is in Los Angeles and doesn't know that you've moved to New York."

"Great, that's still not comforting," Annika grumbled and ended the call. How the fuck is that possible? At least her stalker was still behind bars tonight.

Annika was spent. All she was left with was a hollow emptiness and a queasy stomach. She hesitated before crawling under the covers to sleep, wondering whether to call her parents but deciding against it. All that would do was upset them, and she did not have the energy to deal with any of it.

Maybe with the rising sun, she'd find the strength to focus on what comes next.

EARLY ON SATURDAY, KANE entered the opulent offices of Behr and Goldstein to meet with Larry while the office was empty. The furniture in the sitting room was covered in a silk fabric in various tones and patterns of gold and burgundy. The light fixtures were beautifully crafted from handblown glass. A display of wealth, success, and competence before you even met with an attorney. In many ways, his father had helped Walter and Barry build this firm from a long-standing partnership in both personal and business matters.

He and Larry Behr had grown up together, moving in some of the same social circles during their youth. While Larry understood the demands and expectations that came with being heirs to billionaire families, they forged an early friendship out of their shared efforts to navigate the pressures that came with this lifestyle.

"Hey, Larry," Kane said, poking his head into his office.

Even on the weekend, Larry dressed in a three-piece suit with his signature cufflinks. His fingers filtered through papers neatly aligned in different file folders that one of his assistants or paralegals had left on his desk. "Dude, you got me up this early and didn't even bring coffee? You're not a good friend. I've changed my mind."

"Nope, but what I'm about to talk to you about isn't pleasant. This is to put you on retainer, so what we discussed this morning is protected under the attorney-client privilege." Kane reached into his pocket to retrieve a hundred-dollar bill. When he sat down across from Larry, he tossed the folded bill at him. "It's personal, Larry. If you don't want to be involved, tell me now, and we can forget about this meeting. If you agree, this must stay between us. No one else in this firm can know."

Larry took the bill and stuffed it into his vest pocket. "I assume this is about your father."

"Yes, but this goes much deeper than that." Kane brought Larry up to speed on Bruce's machinations and Walter's own enablement of the situation.

When he finished, Larry's eyebrows lifted. "You think my father and your dad are doing illegal activities? Lines are blurred with wealth, and I'll agree that meddling with that loan crossed that line, but you let them off when you accepted your dad's counter without a second thought."

"I regret it, but I honestly didn't think my father would orchestrate such an egregious abuse of the law with his attorney standing next to him that day. Considering the Montana case, it's highly probable that this isn't their first time bending rules and laws to achieve their goals."

His friend stared at him grimly.

"I need a copy of those executed NDAs," Kane urged. "We both know those documents are keeping something hidden, especially if payments were involved. Craig is looking into this, but I don't know if he'll have time."

Larry rubbed his forehead. "Why won't Craig have time?"

"Since I won't marry Samantha, Dad threatened to terminate his employment and eliminate him from all succession planning. I can't let that happen. I need to find an angle to get my father to step down if one exists. It's time for a change in PCM, and Craig is the right man for that job. You know it and so do I."

"If those NDAs were used to conceal illegal activity or obstruct justice, that would put our firm at risk," Larry said. "I can't see my father risking his reputation. He isn't the type of man. But I'll see what information I can find out."

"I know this is hard, but I appreciate your support." Kane understood how difficult it was to know that your father might be morally compromised and willing to commit a crime for personal gain.

When he reached his building, he parked his Porsche in his underground parking space. He needed to apologize to Annika for his behavior last night. He had not been able to see past his anger or stop to explain anything to her. She might leave after hearing what he planned to tell her, but he would not hide the truth from her. If they were going to be a couple, she had to understand that being a Miller was not always easy.

Hours later, Kane flicked his wrist to check the time. He had not left his couch since he returned home to an empty home, since finding out that Annika had left him. When he gave up refilling his glass, he started drinking straight from the bottle. He still gripped the note he had found. Maybe if he kept holding it, Annika would come back.

He had practically shoved her out of the house by giving her the cold shoulder. Everything happened so fast, but the fact that she left a note without talking to him rankled. She did not even fight for him. Isn't this what he wanted? To remove her from the path of the incoming storm?

He scrubbed his hand down his face. Grabbing his phone to glance at the screen when it beeped with an incoming text from Trent.

Some good news, Penelope's broken neck was caused by a car accident. She wasn't wearing her seatbelt.

His father had better watch his back because he vowed to take him down.

Seventeen

RAZOR BLADES OF LIGHT sliced into Kane's head. He buried his head underneath the pillow, cursing to himself because he forgot to close the window shades.

How did one woman capture his entire being so wholly? He missed her quirky sense of humor, funny ideas, and her devotion to those she cared about. At this moment, he really hated hindsight. God, he had fucked everything up.

Determined to force his father to resign, so his brother could take over as Chief Executive Officer, he showered and dressed for the day. As he headed to the kitchen for caffeine, his cell phone vibrated.

He picked up. "What is it?"

"What crawled up your ass?" Trent asked.

"Dad laid down the gauntlet. He's threatening to fire Craig. He has grown reckless and crossed the line. All of this needs to stop. I'm going to meet with Craig in a bit to start discussing strategy on how to force him into retirement."

"He won't be easy to crack," Trent said.

"I know." Kane blew out a hot breath. "It's going to come down to how we present the evidence and how good we are at bluffing until we get him to admit wrongdoing."

"Okay, I still haven't released the autopsy results to the media yet. I wanted to see if Noah and Larry found anything on the NDAs before I showed our hand, but I need to do it sooner rather than later."

Kane felt a lump in his throat. "And, so you know, I fucked up the other night. Annika left, and I don't know where she's staying now."

Right as Trent started to speak, Kane's phone beeped with an incoming call. Through gritted teeth, he said, "Hey, Craig's on the other line. I've got to go."

The moment he answered the other line, his brother laid into him. "Dad has lost his fucking mind. He's following through on firing me and announcing his revised succession plan to the board next week."

"I'm sorry that he's punishing you because of me. You don't deserve his wrath," Kane said guiltily.

"I don't blame you, Kane," his brother responded.

"I suspect he's also gotten comfortable with bending rules and people's will," Kane offered. "Whatever happened between him and Thomas has rattled him. It seems that Walter is tied to this cyclone too, so Larry's now in the loop."

"How'd Larry handle it? I'm sure it had to be difficult to hear, considering how much he admires his father." Some of the fire left Craig's tone.

"He's leery, but he's trying to access his father's archives for copies of the NDAs. I'm sure he's probably hoping there's a logical explanation. His relationship with his father varied from ours. If this does go south, it'll devastate him." Kane riffled through pages of notes before he continued. "For peace of mind, I asked Noah to access Penelope's records from her accident. He did confirm that she died from a broken neck sustained during the car accident. She wasn't wearing her seat belt. No evidence of foul play."

Craig let out a breath. "I guess that's a relief. I'm not going to lie, my mind went there, Kane."

"I'm with you. Either Dad or Thomas is behind the reporter's death. They're the only two people who directly benefit from the release of that information. I think we keep threading together all the facts until we've got his attention, then we force him to resign on the spot. I want to have Larry there to execute and to navigate any legal hurdles Dad might try to toss out."

"I like it, but there's no guarantee that we'll be successful. Let's hope Larry finds that NDA. That could end this whole clusterfuck."

"High risk, high reward, right, Craig?"

"Damn straight, little brother. Who knew you were so shrewd?" his brother mused.

"Time is of the essence because we need to do this before he can speak to the board. On Tuesday morning, let's review everything we know again," Kane said.

After the call, Kane spent the next few hours reviewing his notes and preparing a bulleted list. Preparation was key, along with being crisp on delivery. As the hours ticked by, he thought Annika might try to reach out to him. His irritation grew when she hadn't. He made one mistake, albeit a big one, but she packed up and walked right out of his life.

Kane's phone buzzed again, and when he looked at the screen, he smiled. "Miss me, Larry?"

"I'm still trying to track down the NDA, but I found something else while I was digging. Remember the other day when I told you how the investigator mentioned Annika's name? Turns out, your father did order the investigation into Annika Bauer. However, there's another name in my dad's notes, a Mike Folley. Do you know him?"

"Yeah, he's Annika's stalker," Kane answered. A sliver of dread settled in his stomach as his father's earlier words echoed in his head.

This olive branch is simply a way to salvage your mistake and prevent others from getting hurt.

"My dad wrote a memo asking our new partnership branch in Los Angeles to fast-track Folley's case to determine whether he's a candidate for early release or home arrest due to overcrowding. He also asked that they offer help pro bono but to send all billable hours and expenses to him for reimbursement."

"I've got to call Trent. Do me a favor and call Craig. He needs to know this." Kane's blood ran cold. "And, Larry, find that NDA. Talk to you tomorrow."

Kane pressed the button for Trent's number, skipping the pleasantries when he answered. "Larry found out that his father worked to get Mike Folley transferred to home arrest for the remainder of his sentence. Can Noah verify that for me?"

"Hold on, let me see if he can chat," Trent said. Then the line went silent while he contacted Noah. After a few minutes, he announced Noah's addition to the line.

"Hey, Kane. Yes, I'm seeing that Folley was moved into home custody late Saturday night. He'll be wearing an ankle monitor that we can track through the system, and will have check-ins, so he won't be going anywhere," Noah supplied, the sound of rapid clicking against a keyboard in the background.

"Noah has a point, but he's still incarcerated. He's got an ankle monitor and doesn't know where Annika lives, with limited means to get to New York," Trent added.

Kane carved his hand through his hair. "Fuck, this is all my dad's doing. What's his angle? Just to force me into marrying Samantha?"

"That's my take. He's using your feelings for Annika to make it happen."

"Does Annika know her stalker has been transferred?" Kane asked.

"Yes, the victim usually gets these updates from their lawyer," Noah answered. "Hey, I've got to run to a meeting, but I'll set an alert on his file. If anything happens, I'll get an update."

"Thanks, Noah," Kane answered.

"Why don't you try calling Annika?" Trent asked once Noah dropped from the line.

Kane bristled. "To say what? I'm sorry, my father is a dick?"

"Yes, for starters. Then you could make sure she's okay, and maybe have a conversation," Trent said.

"I'm the last person she wants to hear from. She left me without saying a word and hasn't even reached out once. That's a pretty direct message," Kane barked, hating how he sounded.

"Get over it and call her," Trent shot back. "If she doesn't want to talk to you, she won't answer, but if she does, then start from there."

"I'll think about it," Kane grumbled as they hung up.

God, he was an ass, and she deserved better. Kane's finger hovered over Annika's number. He desperately wanted to hear her voice, to remind her that she wasn't alone, but his father had to be dealt with to keep everyone safe. Instead, he clicked the button to turn off his screen. He would text her tomorrow after he met with his father. He could try to apologize if she would let him.

Then, in the next breath, he groaned. Maybe he should just call her now?

On Monday morning, Annika dragged herself out of the hotel because she needed to go furniture shopping. It beat spending the day cooped up in her room to dwell on everything in her life she couldn't control. No matter how she looked at the situation, she was mad at herself for abandoning Kane. She told herself she left it to protect him, but in hindsight, it was the wrong approach. She did not give him the courtesy of a face-to-face conversation regarding her decision to leave. It had been easier to chicken out of talking because she'd been afraid he might have persuaded her not to leave altogether.

She raised her hand and hailed an approaching taxi. Sliding into the backseat, she gave the driver the address and then sat back. As she watched the scenery pass, it reminded her of being in a snow globe minus the falling snow. She missed Mill Creek, the town, the mountain views, and all those good memories, but she started to realize she liked New York City, too. She could think of it as home. She was eager to see Central Park when the leaves changed into stunning colors, and to experience her first snowfall. Los Angeles had seasons, but they were nothing compared to the East Coast.

The ring from her cell phone filtered through the cab, competing with the loud advertisements playing on the small screen attached to the headrest. She glanced down, then grimaced at the sight of Trent's name. He had called earlier, and she avoided him by sending it to voicemail.

She hit the green icon. "Hi, I'm sorry, I didn't return your call earlier. It's complicated."

"Ten-fifty, miss," the taxi driver called out to his right shoulder.

"Trent, hold on a second," she instructed, then pulled some cash out of her wallet to settle the fare and tip. "I'm back, how are you?"

"I'm good. Is your complication tied to Kane?" Trent asked.

Annika hesitated, her resolve deflating like the air in her lungs. He might not understand her decision, but she had acted out of love. "Yes. I think it's for the best. Destroying a family isn't an achievement I want."

Trent paused for a moment before he replied. "I'm not taking sides, but maybe you two should talk? Whatever happened between you and Kane doesn't change the fact that we're friends, Annika. I hope you know that."

She smiled at the warmth of his words. "I was a little worried, but I should have known better."

"Anyway, I didn't call to needle you with my excellent relationship counseling. I'm not sure if you've been told about Folley being moved to home arrest for the remainder of his sentence?"

"Yeah, my lawyer told me the other night. I'm not happy about it. I mean...it doesn't seem right or fair."

"It's not, but that's the system. Noah found out that he was transferred out of prison last night. He'll keep monitoring his activity, so you'll have peace of mind."

"Please give Noah my thanks. It does make me feel better. I appreciate the call, Trent."

She slid her phone into her purse pocket with a slight sense of relief that he was being monitored by people she trusted. At least with Folley not knowing she had moved to New York, those thousands of miles that separated them helped too. Blowing the air out of her lungs, she forced her legs to move toward the store. She had furniture to buy and an apartment to clean.

The furniture store took longer than she had expected, but she finally got several pieces to replace the broken ones, and the store agreed to hold the delivery until she secured a new unit. She would tackle apartment hunting tomorrow. Today, she had to begin clearing out all the debris from her studio. The building manager had said he'd place three large plastic trash cans inside to support her efforts, which she appreciated.

Fear snaked down her spine as she stood outside her building. She shook off the sensation and trudged forward toward her unit. When the elevator door slid open, she charged forward, determined to prove to herself that this would not defeat her, either. Her heartbeat increased with each step she took toward her front door. Key in hand, she slid it into the lock and twisted until it clicked.

She squared her shoulders and pushed the door open.

The scent of fresh paint, mixed with the aromas of garlic and bread from the Italian restaurant downstairs, struck her nose. She double-checked the door to ensure it was locked, then flipped her futon over to create a seat. The cushions were slashed, but at least they held her weight. It dawned on her that she had not contacted the dealership about her Fiat or repaid Kane. That went to the top of her priority list.

She reexamined the small area to decide where to start, thankful for renter's insurance, then snapped pictures for her insurance claim that would accompany the police report. She made a note to buy some work gloves on her way back to the hotel tonight to protect her hands from all the broken plates and glass in her kitchen. Then she pulled a folded tote bag from her other bag and focused on gathering her clothing, bedding, and bathroom items.

After a few hours, she twisted off the cap on a bottle of water and took a break. She had made decent progress, but would need another day or two to finish the cleanup. At one point, she considered hiring people to assist her, only to realize she did not want to explain to strangers what had happened. She opened a list app on her phone and added packing boxes and tape to her shopping list.

Her phone vibrated in her hand. She wanted to speak to her parents, but they had been through so much. She did not want to worry them by letting them know everything that was going on. She hit the end button and sent the call to voicemail, making a note to update them after she moved.

Her finger hovered over the photo icon. When she pressed the dot, she smiled at her recent pictures from Mill Creek. One of her favorites was of Kane and Leah splashing in the creek while he wore the shorts she had made for him. She flicked to the picture of him holding his first mud pie, his smile so genuine.

Her heart wrenched as the first sob escaped her mouth. She did not know if she would ever get over him. She sobbed for her past, the crappy present, and what would be missing from her future.

January—Current Day

Mill Creek

JASMINE WENT TO THE bathroom to grab the tissue box, handing one to Annika before leaning down to hug her.

"I'm so sorry, Annika. How horrible. What is it with fathers who are also assholes?" Jasmine said in a quiet voice. "Noah's father caused him so much heartache, and now he's stuck in a state of limbo as he sorts through how he feels about him."

"In my experience, power, real or perceived, screws people up," Aimee added.

"That's true." Jasmine nodded. "Sometimes it isn't even a person who abuses it. An organization can do it just as easily."

Annika dabbed her eyes. "Isn't it funny? I lived through all of this, and I even know how it ends, but here I am crying."

"Shh, be you and let the rest of us just hold on and love you," Maggie said soothingly.

The moment was interrupted when a ruckus erupted in the kitchen, followed by loud booming voices.

"Maggie, grab the first aid kit. Kane used his head instead of the glove," Trent hollered.

"Oh my God," Annika gasped, bolting upward towards the kitchen. Jasmine, Aimee, and Maggie were on her heels.

"Dude, when you catch flying objects, it helps if your eyes are open," Clarke said, bending over Kane to examine his knot.

"Did you win to make that bruise worth it at least?" Aimee asked, peering around Clarke.

"That's my girl! Always has her eye on the score." Clark beamed, turning around to lift her up into his lap as he took a seat at the kitchen table next to Kane.

Noah tucked his arm around Jasmine and tugged her against his side. "Statistically, we had a great chance at winning. We were in the lead by three runs."

When Maggie returned from the laundry room, her husband took the big red first aid kit from her and stepped in front of Kane. Trent tore open one of the antiseptic wipes to cleanse the scrape just over his friend's eyebrow.

"Holy hell, that burns," Kane grumbled.

Annika leaned over him, gently blowing on the area to ease the pain. "Aww, poor baby."

Kane gave her his best pouty face. "Kisses would make this feel a lot better."

Trent applied a bandage, then handed Kane an icepack for his bump. "Good news, you're fine. Bad news, it's definitely going to bruise, but you'll look cool."

"So, how'd the game end?" Aimee prompted.

"Oh, right, sorry. I got sidetracked with Kane's medical care." Noah let out a grunt when Jasmine elbowed him.

"Be nice," Jasmine said, pointing her finger at him.

Trent jumped in. "The bases were loaded. The pitch count was three to two. And when the batter popped the ball up, it went into right field, where Kane was playing. Kane did his best, running forward with his arm up in the air, and we thought he was going to catch the ball. Only, he closed his eyes right before the ball landed."

Clarke chuckled, picking up the story next. "Instead of the ball hitting the pocket, it biffed the top of his glove and ricocheted off his face before hitting the ground. So, all runners advanced and we lost the game."

"That's horrible. Isn't there a do-over or some rule that you only get one run?" Maggie asked. "There was an injury on the play."

"Nope, Glove-Face cost us the game," Clarke bellyached as Kane flashed him a middle finger.

While everyone continued to chat about the game, Kane winked at Annika. "You okay, sweetheart? Your eyes are red."

She beamed down on him. "I'm fine. I'm finally telling the girls how we met, and tears happened."

Kane tugged Annika closer and pressed a kiss against her forehead. "You amaze me every day."

"We didn't mean to crash your party, but we figured we should patch Kane up before we head to Two-Stepping for beers and food. Ladies, are you interested in joining us?" Trent asked.

"You boys skedaddle. We're..." Aimee stood, cocking her hip to the side as she pointed at her friends and then herself. "Bonding. It's a boobs-only meeting."

"I love boobs," Clarke muttered.

She gently swatted her husband as she shooed all the men out of the house. "I know. You'll get to see them later, big guy. Now go and drink away your sorrows with the boys."

After the guys left, they stayed in the kitchen, exchanging champagne for water. Annika couldn't believe it had taken her this long to share any of this with her friends, but it felt cathartic. Now, it's time for the grand finale.

Eighteen

June—Six Months Earlier

New York City

EARLY TUESDAY MORNING, KANE sat on a call with Craig, Noah, Trent, and Larry, to review the plan for their surprise meeting with his father today. This meeting would be incredibly difficult, knowing that their solution was not a quick hit but rather a series of blows. They needed to stoke Bruce's anger so that when he faltered, they could nail his ass to the wall. From there, they could move for an immediate resignation, thus limiting the irreparable damage he was causing, and move Craig to his rightful position as the new CEO.

If they failed, pursuing the criminal route would take longer.

"Are we all in agreement that my father grossly and egregiously abused his position of power as CEO, and that Walter, as his legal representation, was complicit?" Kane asked, waiting for everyone to respond.

"Constructing the agreement is key. The NDA should be the last piece you drop," Larry interjected. At the final hour of the night before, he finally located the NDAs on his father's personal hard drive.

"Bruce will be startled that you know, which will hopefully make him reassess how much proof you have for the previous discussion points.

"My team will continue their investigation into the murder of Melvin Wilcox," Trent chimed in. "Since the incident crossed state lines, we were able to partner with the FBI on it. Noah has already started lending his expertise and analytical support."

"All right. It's now or never. Kane and Larry, I'll meet you in PCM's lobby. Trent and Noah, thank you for all your support," Craig said right before he ended the call.

A couple of hours later, Kane drove into the garage at PCM, zipping into a parking spot before heading into the building. He was wound tighter than a spring, ready to burst. When he saw his brother and Larry, he nodded and joined them in the elevator, where they stood in companionable silence. He couldn't count the number of times he had ridden in this car as a child, but today was the first time he felt in control of his life.

When the elevator doors opened, he took a deep breath to center his mind and still his body. His father's assistant was not at her desk yet, which meant they had the element of surprise on their side. Craig opened the office door to allow entry into his father's kingdom, where they found him standing behind his desk, looking out the floor-to-ceiling windows.

Kane had stood at those same windows many times himself and knew the view of Battery Park and the harbor well. He thought about the amount of time Bruce had spent in this office, working to ensure PCM thrived, rather than with his family.

"Jenna, I thought you were taking today off?" Bruce asked, his tone distant as he stared straight ahead.

"I believe she did," Kane answered as he took a seat in one of the chairs facing his father's desk. He sat back and crossed his leg, resting his ankle on his knee. Craig took the other seat while Larry brought over a chair from the conference table in the corner. When his father turned to face him, his face revealed nothing until he saw that Craig and Larry were also present.

"Larry, I don't believe you're on my calendar today," Bruce commented, his finger reviewing his daily schedule, line by line.

"We're here to bring some concerning information to your attention and to discuss a mitigation plan," Craig said. "We're concerned about your affiliation with Thomas Monroe, who we have learned has a criminal record."

Bruce waved his hand dismissively. "Do a public search, and I think you'll discover the truth that he has no such thing, which makes mitigation irrelevant."

"Huh, that's interesting because we know background checks are part of your vetting process," Kane said, turning his head to Larry. "Perhaps you didn't do a thorough enough investigation, because Larry found several very criminal charges, including driving under the influence, disorderly conduct, and aggravated assault. Isn't that right?"

"Behr & Goldstein has one of the best investigators in the business. But you know that, Mr. Miller," Larry answered.

Bruce's eyes narrowed as the muscle at his jaw clenched. "Why are the three of you here?"

"Since you have demanded that Kane marry Thomas Monroe's daughter, we want to know if you were aware of his criminal background," Craig chimed in, his voice firm. "This type of information could negatively impact PCM, especially because you're one of the largest donors to his presidential campaign."

Kane raised his hands wide. "Imagine the press reports: Billionaire Bruce Miller Backs Known Criminal. Scratch that—Billionaire Bruce Miller Tries to Buy the Presidency."

"How scandalous," Craig added.

Bruce's calm demeanor slipped. He pointed his finger at Kane and then Craig. "I had no fucking clue. Those records were sealed. Who did you learn this information from?"

Kane swallowed and inhaled slowly through his nose. He was about to deliver the first bluff, and he hoped like hell his father would take the bait. "Penelope's father, Judge Jerry Whitehall. You know, the very same judge who sealed those records."

"This meeting is over." Bruce shoved his chair back and stood. "Your insinuations are baseless."

"All those NDAs overseen by Walter in Montana tell a different story," Kane pressed. He ignored his phone vibrating in his pocket.

Larry held up a copy of one of the NDAs. "There are many just like this one."

Craig looked over at Larry. "Who signed that one?"

"The rancher who hired Thomas Monroe to represent him against PCM, but that case was dismissed due to lack of evidence by none other than Judge Whitehall," Larry read from the document.

"Look at all those coincidences. Then, when we factor in the accounting trail for those stipends, it looks pretty suspicious. I wonder what the media will say when they get hold of all of this," Craig said, shaking his head.

"You would risk destroying PCM based on false conclusions," his father spat, the vein on his forehead now visible.

"These are facts, Dad," Craig challenged.

Kane's muscles relaxed for the first time in a few days. They were so close to achieving their goal. He put his leg down and bent forward, resting his arms on his knees to stare his father right in the eye as he delivered the one-two punch. If this assumption failed, Craig was prepared to spin the argument toward Thomas and how he wanted to take down PCM and their father.

"It's only a matter of time before it all comes out, Dad. Melvin Wilcox, an investigative reporter looking into the PCM lawsuit, didn't die from a mere auto accident in Mill Creek. His neck had been broken before the accident, as confirmed by the local medical examiner. Trent's team found his thumb drive of incriminating evidence, which was left behind when the rest of his work documents were taken from his car."

"So what? That doesn't mean shit." Bruce's tone dripped with contempt.

"It would if PCM benefits from him being silenced. It's convenient that the company jet you set to pick me up in Boise landed the night before the reporter's death. What would the passenger manifest show? Could the pilots or attendants report under oath that it was an empty flight?"

"That man had to die because he wouldn't stop. This would have buried PCM," Bruce roared, shifting to Craig. "And you... You have no fucking clue the sacrifices involved in running a global conglomerate, you fucking imbecile."

A heavy silence blanketed the room.

Craig spoke first. His tone was calm and even. "Dad, you've given your life to this company—"

"Yes, I have! It's about damn time that you understand that difficult choices must be made," Bruce said in a smug voice.

Craig put his hand up, continuing slowly. "And to continue its legacy, it's time for you to step down. Murder is not acceptable for any reason, and that decision alone makes you unfit to continue running this company."

Larry sifted through a few documents in his folder until he found the ones he wanted and handed them to Bruce. "The first document is your official resignation letter from PCM, effective immediately. Craig Miller is taking over as the new Chief Executive Officer, as outlined in your succession plan. The second is a press announcement about your resignation and Craig's new position in the company."

Kane handed the pen to his father. His phone once again vibrated in his pocket, but he could not afford to answer it now.

"Why should I do this?" Bruce asked in a defiant voice. "I'm calling Walter."

Larry leaned forward. "Listen, you asshole. You destroyed my father in the process of protecting your empire. I have already had a similar discussion with him, and as of last night, he is retired. Together, we prepared a list of illegal or heavily questionable legal matters that fall under current or future timeframes. As you know, the attorney-client privilege is not valid, and my father is prepared to be deposed and will seek immunity."

"It's over, Dad. Do you want to blow up all that you built, or will you act swiftly and give me a chance to lead us through this dark moment?" Craig asked.

Bruce yanked a pen out of the display on his desk and scrawled his name on each page. Kane closed his eyes for a moment, relieved that they got him to agree. It was a short-lived reprieve when his phone buzzed again. He yanked it from his pocket and read Trent's text, which made his blood run cold.

Annika's stalker is in NYC. Call me NOW. We can't get a hold of her.

Kane whirled on his father. "You son of a bitch. I know you and Walter were behind getting Annika's stalker out of prison. You'd better hope she's safe."

"Go, Kane. I'll finish this up here," Craig replied.

"Call Trent!" Kane called as he raced out of the office.

All of this had been set in motion because his father was a greedy and controlling bastard.

All Kane cared about, all he ever wanted, was to have Annika back in his life, safe and sound. He loved her. He would do whatever it took to change her mind and make her his wife. When he tried calling Trent's number, it went to voicemail. Annika's number did the same.

Once he reached the lobby, he ran toward his car and started driving like a madman toward her apartment, maneuvering in and out of traffic as fast as he could through the streets of New York without endangering anyone's safety. His heart hammered inside his chest as he thought about Annika.

He pressed the phone button on his steering wheel and commanded his automated system to dial Trent's number. When his friend's voice echoed in the car, a brief wave of relief washed over him. "Where is Annika? Is she okay?"

Trent got to the point without preamble. "Folley cut off his ankle monitor last night. There was no new financial activity, so the search grid remained localized. After a few hours, with no sign of him, the FBI started expanding its search. His name hasn't been found on any airline passenger manifests, but facial recognition picked him up at LaGuardia airport. He hasn't been seen since the airport. NYPD has been alerted and is coordinating search efforts to locate and apprehend him. Officers have been dispatched to the apartment.

"I'd put money on my father being behind all of this and flew him in on one of the company jets," Kane gritted out. "Folley has been in the city for a while. What if he took her somewhere?"

"Don't go there. Annika is smart and strong," Trent said calmly. "As soon as you arrive, tell the police you're her fiancé."

"I'll call you when I know something." Kane hung up as he slammed his gearshift into park. Relieved to see the police were on scene and setting up a perimeter with barricades and yellow tape, he jogged toward a group of officers who had gathered on the sidewalk outside her building, with his heart lodged in his throat.

ANNIKA DECIDED TO GREET Tuesday morning head-on by getting an early start. On her way to her apartment, she stopped at the bakery on the ground floor of her building to purchase a bagel and a cup of coffee. It was time to put this place in her rearview mirror.

She slid her key into the lock and entered. First, she needed to catch up on a few bills, and then she'd get started. She sat on the futon and started to grab her computer from her bag when there was a knock at her front door. Maybe it was her superintendent wanting to make sure she was happy with the repairs.

She peered through the peephole and gasped in horror.

Please, please, please, let this be a trick her mind was playing on her. Her body shook on unsteady legs, causing her to sway and use the door to balance her weight. When her eyes didn't lie for the second time, she looked through the peephole, and a guttural groan escaped her lips.

How could this be happening?

Her vision blurred as the hot tears streamed down her face. Her heart thundered in her chest, making it difficult to think. She needed to call for help. Her will to survive straightened her spine. Her eyes darted around the studio in search of her cell phone. Staring at her target, she launched herself toward her lifeline and forced her leaden legs to propel her forward.

As Annika raced for her purse, she heard a loud bang and splintering wood. The hairs on the back of her neck stood at attention as heavy footsteps bore down on her.

She had to get to her phone. It was the last thought she registered before a heavy, unyielding weight slammed into her back, forcing her to the ground. The air whooshed from her lungs as panic overtook her body. She kicked and twisted, trying to free herself, but Mike Folley didn't budge.

He grabbed both of her arms with considerable force and pulled them behind her back until the backs of her wrists touched. Something slid against her skin before a sharp zipping sound pierced her ears. He yanked the plastic hard enough that it cut sharply into her skin. Folley leaned forward and whispered in her ear. "If you scream, you'll regret it. Be a good girl, and I'll give you a treat."

"Yes," she croaked.

He nipped her earlobe before easing off her body. He hauled her up to stand on her feet before shoving her roughly toward the futon. "What the hell happened in here?"

"Someone broke in a few days ago," she answered. She rolled onto her side and saw him peering right and left down her hallway. Silently, she hoped someone had heard the commotion and called the police.

"I'm curious—did you miss me?" he asked as he picked up loose pieces of wood lying on the floor outside her front door. He righted the door as best he could, but it still looked as if she had left it ajar.

The broken pieces would only draw attention if someone took a closer look.

Not at all. In fact, I had hoped you would never be released from jail.

"Shouldn't you be in Los Angeles?" What was he planning to do to her? What did he want?

She felt perspiration dotting her forehead. The pain in her shoulders made it difficult to concentrate. Fear coiled like a snake around her body when he moved closer to her. She hated showing him her fear. The last thing she wanted to do was give him the satisfaction.

How had he escaped? Had he removed his ankle monitor? She tilted her head a little to see if she could spot the device, but he was wearing pants.

His face twisted into a satisfied look. "I love watching your lips tremble."

Since he didn't answer her question about Los Angeles, she tried a different tack. "How did you know I was here...in New York?"

Her face exploded in pain as he smacked her hard. "I'm asking the questions, not you."

Tears stung her eyes as every nerve ending in her cheek flared to life. "I'm sorry. I'm just shocked to see you after all this time."

"You made a difference in my life. I looked forward to every session. As our bond deepened, I'd realized we are meant to be together...forever. So, imagine my surprise and heartache when you stopped being a part of our group. You didn't like my gifts. You cast me aside like yesterday's garbage. You ripped my fucking heart from my chest," he spat, spittle covering her face.

Annika decided she had to try to make him understand her actions. "I never meant to cause you distress. I didn't want to give you the wrong impression by not reciprocating your feelings, so I removed myself from your session. I'm sorry, my actions hurt you."

A smug smile lifted the corner of his lips. "It seems the universe agreed, because it led me straight to you."

Annika twisted and pulled at her hands, trying to free them from the bindings. Instead, all she managed was to dig the restraints deeper into her flesh, causing more pain and blood. She wasn't going to slip free of these plastic ties. She needed to buy herself more time, forcing herself to engage. As long as his mouth moved, she had a chance to survive.

And if she survived, she promised herself that after she apologized for leaving Kane, the stupid note instead of talking to him, she would also tell him that she loved him.

"What do you mean you were led to me?" she asked, forcing steel into her voice. She drew a deep breath through her nose, held it for a few seconds, and then exhaled slowly to calm herself. She refused to give him any satisfaction by showing her distress.

Folley lifted her head higher so he could look into her eyes, to see her reaction to whatever he was about to say next. He rolled his eyes at her question. "I've already told you...fate! One day, this new high-dollar lawyer met with me and got me moved to house arrest. Once I was home, I found an envelope under my pillow with everything I needed to bring us together. It contained photos, your address, cash, and instructions guiding me to a private plane that would take me to New York."

Who would do that to her? One person jumped to the forefront of her mind: Bruce Miller. Caroline had warned her that she was concerned about how far her husband would go to protect PCM and his family. Annika fought the panic that threatened to shut down her brain. She had to keep him talking, but her stomach churned.

"You were lucky that you never had to go to a foster home," Folley said. "Passed from home to home, constantly rejected, bullied, and told you were a bad child." She startled when he put his head in her lap, wrapping his arms around her waist. "Everything changed when you became my therapist. I found my special someone who understood and accepted me. You loved me."

Annika bounced her knees up and down to interrupt his delusional stroll down memory lane. "I do care and want you to get the help you deserve. You've broken some laws by coming here, but if you surrender peacefully, I'll speak to the authorities on your behalf."

Mike's head immediately popped up, and his eyes burned with rage. "Shut up! Shut the hell up! I'm not going to watch you hand me off again. If I have to go back to jail, then neither of us is making it out of here alive."

Annika realized her mistake. Her time had run out, and so had her options. Terror washed over her when she saw him draw a long, partially serrated knife from a sheath attached to his belt.

This was not how she was supposed to die.

Nineteen

A SPARK OF HOPE flared deep in Annika's stomach as she heard sirens. She forced down her mortal fear. To give the police time to do their jobs, she had to get Folley to see the mistake he was about to make.

The press of cold steel against her cheek interrupted her train of thought. When the blade trailed down her neck and then lower until it rested on top of her knee, her body trembled. Her tormentor smiled, then sawed the knife back and forth lightly across the top of her pant-clad knee.

"Leave now, and you can escape before the police arrive," she pleaded. "I know you heard the sirens."

He continued the back-and-forth motion with the blade. His head hung low. "No, I'm where I want to be. This is fate."

"It can't be fate if we die." Annika hissed out in pain when the knife sliced into her left leg. Blood seeped between the fabric and her leg.

When Folley lifted his face to look at her, his eyes were dark and empty, and his laugh was pure evil. He removed the knife from her leg and walked behind her. "Your listening skills are pathetic for a supposed therapist. I told you that we are going to be together forever."

She refused to die now, after everything that she'd survived. In these final moments, she wasn't sure which was worse—not knowing when he would make the fatal strike or knowing she would never get to see the people she loved again. Desperation fueled her actions as she twisted her body to look at her stalker.

"What if we decided to live together...away from everyone...just the two of us?" she asked, pushing the words through the lump in her throat.

"Don't lie, Annika. No one likes a liar."

She gasped as the sting of the knife's blade landed just under her jawbone, nicking her delicate skin. Tears slid down her cheeks. She was terrified of what would come next. Closing her eyes, she pictured Kane standing in front of her, his handsome face smiling as he told her to stay strong and fight for him. She felt her parents' unwavering love surrounding her, giving her the strength to dig deep and not give up.

Folley scraped the blade up and down in a shaving motion. "Beg for your life...for my forgiveness... If it's sweet enough, it could be the difference between a long and a quick death."

She might not have been able to control how her body reacted to fear, but she would be damned if she begged this asshole for anything. Her thoughts drifted back to Kane, and she wished she had told him she loved him. How she wished they had had a future together.

Chaos erupted all around her as a loud voice started shouting several commands. "Drop the knife, put your hands in the air, and step away from the woman!"

Immense pain radiated around the top of her shoulder as she felt the tip of the knife sink in. Unable to stop her reaction to the pain, she screamed.

Gunshots split the air, followed by a loud grunt. The knife clattered to the ground. Her stalker's lifeless body crushed her into the futon, weighing her down. The police barked more commands as they stormed into her small studio.

Annika snapped her eyes open. Her ears rang. The body was lifted away from her, and she scrambled away from her stalker.

"Annika Bauer?" one of the officers asked her while the others slowly approached with guns drawn.

"Yes?" she answered.

An officer leaned down and pressed two fingers into Folley's neck. He shook his head as he declared, "No pulse."

"Are you sure he's dead?" she whispered. She held her breath, afraid he might jump back into action.

"Yes, Ms. Bauer," the officer next to her answered before thumbing a button on his radio to provide an update. The lead officer made a hand signal, signaling everyone to holster their weapons.

"Please get him away from me," she whispered. Her voice was strangled with emotion. Relief flooded her body at the knowledge that Mike Folley would never hurt her again.

The officer acknowledged her request but held up his gloved hand. "Not yet. We need to process the scene before he's moved. It'll take a few minutes."

Another person approached with a camera, snapping several pictures. Yellow number markers were dropped, and there were more camera clicks. Another officer approached her and took more pictures. Finally, two officers moved him to the floor, covering up his body.

A paramedic appeared practically out of thin air, asking Annika, "Where does it hurt?" She tried to interact, but she felt sluggish. Her brain could not formulate a reply. Her mouth felt like she'd swallowed cotton. Tears streamed down her face as tremors wracked her body.

"You're in shock," the paramedic said. "First, I'm going to cut these zip ties off your wrists. It'll hurt because your blood flow has been restricted and your muscles are tight."

She watched wide-eyed as he showed her the scissors. An officer appeared next to the paramedic with an evidence bag. Loud snips followed, and then the plastic ties were added to the plastic receptacle. The moment her wrists were freed, she yelped in pain as she moved her hands into her lap. Pinpricks of sensation raced from her shoulders to her fingers, igniting a fiery path as her nerves roared back to life.

"Now, I'm going to check you over," the medic explained. "Then, I'm going to tend to your injuries. I want to make sure you know you are safe. Can you nod your head if you understand me?"

She nodded. Her gaze zipped around the room, watching the activity around her. The whole scene was eerily familiar to what she'd experienced in Los Angeles: the photos, the yellow markers, the evidence bags.

"You're doing great. I don't think you'll experience any permanent nerve damage from being restrained. The cuts on your neck are superficial and will heal. The one on your shoulder can be closed with Dermabond. Now, I need to check your wrists and knees. Are there any other places that hurt?"

"No," she managed in a small voice. She looked down at her wrists, which were raw and irritated from the bindings. "Just the obvious."

"This one is the deepest of all and will require suturing." When he finished, the paramedic applied an antiseptic ointment to the wound on the top of her leg before applying a large bandage. Then he dressed her shoulder wound.

After the medic finished, the lead officer and another man approached her. "Ms. Bauer, we'd like to ask you some questions. If this becomes overwhelming, we can always take a break."

She nodded for them to proceed. She had learned in Los Angeles that the fastest way to get this over with was to comply. Then she could get the hell out of this apartment and follow through on her promise to Kane. She needed to warn him about his father.

KANE STOOD AT THE end of Annika's hallway behind a barricade. As Trent had advised him, he announced himself as Annika's fiancé, and he waited for what seemed like hours for the all-clear signal to let him through. He heard updates over the officers' radios that stood around him. He fidgeted, and his skin crawled with the electricity of his impatience.

Another eternity passed before one of the officers told him that Annika had sustained minor injuries but was okay. When the call came that he could go back to her, he rushed down the hallway, needing her in his arms so he could see for himself. He loved her with every fiber of his being and planned to spend every day showing her.

When he entered her tiny unit, his eyes locked on the back of her head. She sat on a broken futon, facing two officers who were questioning her. He moved closer, passing a covered body just off to her side. It was a chilling observation, but he felt satisfied knowing that the bastard was dead. She would never have to face him again.

Annika's head turned, and when her gaze fell on him, she smiled. "Kane."

He let out a huge breath as tears stung his eyes. He tugged her into his arms when she tried to shoot up but swayed on her feet. The steady beat of her heart against his chest and the subtle scents of vanilla and lavender eased his tension. This was his woman, and he would never let go again. As his emotions overwhelmed him, his only priority was to ensure she understood what was in his heart and soul because she now truly owned him.

"I love you, Annika. I never should have shut you out," Kane whispered, as he framed her face in his hands, careful not to hurt her.

"I never should have left that note." Annika's voice cracked. "I'm so sorry. I love you, too."

In that moment, his world righted itself because he knew they would work out their differences together. Kane pulled back from their embrace to press a kiss to her forehead. He tucked her against his side.

"Let's wrap this up so that I can take you home. You'll be lucky if I let you out of my sight for five minutes."

Her smile was full of promise. "I'm not going to complain about that just yet."

Despite everything, he knew they would forge a future together. He listened as she answered the remaining questions and recounted the details of the attack. He disliked the bruises and bandages covering her skin, but she was safe and alive.

"Okay, Ms. Bauer. I think we're finished for now. What's the best number to reach you if we have additional questions?" one of the officers asked as he flipped a page in his notebook to record her information.

A strong urge to protect Annika swelled in Kane as he swept her into his arms. He wanted her out of this apartment and back in his home. He provided the officers with his information. His voice broke with emotion when he added, "I can't thank all of you enough."

The officer patted his shoulder. "It's our job, but we always enjoy a good ending."

Annika turned her head to look up at him. "Can we leave now?"

Once he had her tucked into the passenger seat with her purse, he pressed a kiss to her mouth. As he started the car and pulled into the traffic, he said, "We've got to call Trent."

The moment he answered, Kane gave him the good news. "She's sitting right next to me. Mike Folley is dead."

"Thank God, Annika. How are you holding up?" Trent asked.

"So much better now." She sighed and leaned back into her seat. "Thank you for keeping an eye on me, and please tell Noah I owe him a hug whenever I meet him."

"I don't get a hug? I've known you longer." Trent pouted.

"True. Both of you get hugs." Annika chuckled, but then a look of concern passed over her face. "I think we may still have a problem. Folley mentioned that someone had given him all the information he needed to find me and had arranged a private flight to bring him to New York. I think your dad made all this happen."

"You're right, sweetheart. When we get home, I'll fill you in on everything that's happened," Kane said. His gut tightened at her admission, but the important thing now was that Annika was safe.

Kane had insisted on carrying Annika all the way up to his condominium. In the entryway, he gently set her on her feet and placed his hand at the small of her back to guide her to his family room.

"What do you need, Annika?"

"Just you," she replied. Her nose wrinkled at the memory of Caroline sitting on the sofa next to her not that long ago.

"What's wrong?" Kane asked, immediately squatting down in front of her.

She patted the cushion next to her. "This is where your mom sat on Saturday. She just showed up. She had come to speak with you, but since you weren't home, she spoke with me—or rather, threatened me."

Kane's brows snapped together. "What does that mean?"

"She told me how your father was threatening you and Craig. I didn't want to be the reason either of you suffered, so I left," She crumpled against the couch. "I'm so sorry, Kane. I thought I was making a good choice when I should have told you to your face."

Kane leaned back with her. "That makes two of us. I never should have shut you out. But we finally got him to admit to killing the reporter. We forced him to resign, and as of right now, Craig is the new CEO of PCM."

She listened as Kane told her every detail of how they got Bruce Miller to admit to killing Melvin Wilcox and to step down as head of PCM. She was so angry at the lengths to which that man had gone to keep his power. It was incredible that he could be so cruel to Craig and Kane, yet they still prevailed.

"How is Larry handling all of this?" she asked.

"I get the feeling not well. He looked up to his old man, so I'm sure this is devastating to him."

They sat together in quiet for a few moments before Annika yawned. "Can I take a bath? I want to wash all the ick from today off my body."

Kane pulled her into his arms once again as he stood and didn't stop carrying her until he reached the bathroom.

"You know my legs weren't broken, right?" she asked.

The puzzled look on his face made her smile. "This isn't for you. It's for me, sweetheart. I need to hold you close."

She watched as he turned on the taps to fill the tub with steaming hot water, then started the jets before pulling open a drawer. Soon after, steam started to coat the mirrors, but not before she saw her own reflection, which made her cringe. It also made all her aches and pains flare up. No wonder he was trying to coddle her.

"Here's a waterproof bandage for your knee. You soak and relax while I make you some tea. Holler if you need me," Kane said, the door clicking shut upon his retreat.

Annika removed her clothing, letting it fall on the floor in a pile. She planned to throw out every item. The warm water felt heavenly as it seeped into her tired bones, only stinging her cuts for a moment. She pulled her injured knee toward her chest to keep it mostly out of the water while the jets worked on all her knots. She was pleased that she would never have to worry about that man again.

Pulling the sponge off the ledge, she lathered her body with soap to wash the day's ugliness from her. After rinsing off the suds, she laid her head back on the rolled towel at the tub's edge and closed her eyes. After her soak, she pulled a fluffy white towel from the rack and dried herself. She found Kane's robe on the back of the door, with its faint scent of sandalwood, and wrapped herself in it.

Kane ended his call as he watched her emerge from the bathroom. "How are you feeling? Your tea is on the nightstand."

She took a sip of the chamomile tea and moaned in appreciation. "Where do you want to play doctor?"

His eyes widened for a moment. "Uh, sit on the bed. I'll get the supplies."

When he returned from the bathroom, he had an overabundance of bandages to complete the job. His touch was gentle as he applied ointment and bandages to each wound. Once he finished, he kissed her lips. “I thought we could fly to Mill Creek at the end of the week.”

“That sounds perfect,” she answered, then yawned. She crawled under the covers, popping her eyes open briefly as she heard the rustle of his clothing.

Wearing only his boxer shorts, he carefully folded back the comforter and slid next to her before pulling her into his arms. She loved knowing she was in Kane’s bed. A deep sense of love and contentment wrapped around her, lulling her into a deep sleep.

Twenty

THE FOLLOWING FRIDAY MORNING, Kane rested on his elbow as he watched Annika rest.

"Good morning," she said, her voice heavy from sleep. Her eyes fluttered open. She greeted him with the sweetest smile.

Kane trained his eyes on her, and when her tongue darted out to moisten his lips, he moaned. She revved his engines like no one else. Not only was she a beautiful, intelligent, and sexy woman, but her inner spirit was his life. He rolled on top of her and wiped a few wayward strands of hair off her face.

"I want you, sweetheart." His cock was rock hard.

She craned her neck to look at the clock. "What time's our flight?"

"Whenever I say so," he answered, nipping at her lips.

"I'm not used to flying private," she replied, wrapping her arms around his back.

"I love you," he muttered before he claimed her lips in a slow and seductive dance.

He tugged her nightshirt up off her body. He kissed his way down her torso, nipping and sucking on each nipple, loving the guttural moans that escaped her throat. He sat back on his haunches as he removed his boxers.

Her gaze followed his movements until his cock sprang free. Not once had Annika averted her gaze, and her sharp intake of breath made him groan with anticipation.

"Your body, Kane, is a work of art," she whispered. She shimmied out of her panties, tossing them at him.

He crawled back over her, appreciating the stunning, sun-kissed woman who lay beneath him. He pressed kisses along the thick scars she had on her leg.

"Don't, Kane. It's ugly," she said, trying to pull his attention away from staring at her mangled flesh.

He emitted a low growl deep in his throat before he addressed her inaccurate statement. "All I see is perfection and strength."

A beautiful smile covered her face as her eyes sparkled, all traces of self-doubt gone.

He licked and laved his way up her body until he reached her wet heat and tormented her nubbin until she writhed with satisfaction. Intense ripples of pleasure had her calling out his name. He crawled up further, letting his hand skim over the sensitive skin. Her mewl of delight filled his ears as he continued his slow and methodical torture. He worked her higher until her body unraveled underneath him with her orgasm.

After he sheathed himself, he bent down to leave a series of kisses from her navel to her lips. When she arched her back and moaned, he claimed her mouth in a toe-curling kiss.

"You ready, sweetheart?" he asked.

"Yes," she replied, her eye seductive and bright. "We should try this at a high altitude."

He wasn't a member of that particular club, but with Annika, he wanted a lifetime membership. He continued to slide his way down her body, pressing kisses and leaving light bite marks everywhere he explored. His erection was harder than he could ever remember, and he desperately needed to plunge into her tight heat. He pressed the tip of his cock between her folds, thrusting forward, plunging even deeper. Passion and lust quickened his pace.

Love. Devotion. Forever. These were the words he repeated to himself as he made love to Annika.

Little moans of pleasure escaped her throat as he pushed her body toward climax. His balls tightened as tiny electric pulses raced up his spine. He moved his hand between them and applied pressure to her clit, until her body clenched tight around his cock.

"Let yourself go...I have you," he murmured from above. He loved how her eyes darkened with her arousal and the way her body tensed as her orgasm started to crest.

He thrust into her harder, pushing her over the edge into ecstasy. On his final stroke, he threw his head back and shouted her name as he exploded. A promise to all who could hear that Annika was his forever.

While she showered, Kane called the jewelry store, giving the saleswoman his credit card number and then Albert's name for pickup. He knew Albert would tuck it away on the plane for him. He made one final call to Trent to check in on the progress of the land he was buying.

"Hey, Trent, were you able to get a copy of the deed?" Kane asked.

"Not yet, but if it doesn't record, then I'll make up a temporary one for illustrative purposes."

"Perfect, I appreciate it. I'm going to ask her to marry me in the meadow."

"Congratulations, man! She's perfect for you."

"We'll see you soon," Kane said and then headed toward the shower.

LATER IN THE DAY, they finally pulled into Trent's driveway. Annika burst out of the car and right into Trent's arms, giving him the hug she owed him.

"Thank you for keeping me safe," she said.

"How are you feeling?" Trent asked, pulling her into a bear hug.

"Better every day," Annika answered.

Trent's house looked different from the last time they were here. Plastic tarp covered a large section of the house's exterior and scaffolding had been erected all around the perimeter. Equipment and pallets full of various supplies littered the yard. When they entered the house, furniture had been moved, and boxes were stacked to allow access to the walls and floors.

"Well, I see the renovation is ready to start on Monday," Kane said, right before he threw his duffel into his friend's arms.

"I hope so, because this architect I know told me it's worth all this chaos," Trent said.

Annika giggled, winking at Trent. "Seriously, how are you holding up with this mess?"

"Barely. It's been difficult, especially when the project tries to kill you."

Annika's eyes went wide. "What does that mean?"

Kane shot his friend an exasperated look before he pulled him into a manly backslapping hug. "Seriously, you're going to try and milk that story in front of Annika?"

Trent roared with laughter. "I'm so glad you two are back. I've been damn lonely since you left."

"I'm glad we were missed." Annika elbowed Kane in the gut. "But I want to know what happened."

Trent winked at Kane. "It was a mistake. The scaffolding assembled by the front door didn't have all the pins inserted, and it collapsed in a windstorm."

"Geez, that's terrible. I'm glad you're okay. Is it all fixed now?" Annika asked.

"Yup, and everything is on schedule," Trent said.

Kane started scanning around. "I want to look over the plans and walk the house with you."

"Sure, but let me change out of my uniform," Trent replied as he headed toward his bedroom. "I'll meet you in the kitchen in five minutes."

"While you guys do that, I'm going to sit down by the creek and enjoy what's left of this beautiful day," Annika told Kane, who already had the blueprints unrolled across the kitchen table.

She loved to listen to the creek while taking in the mountain air. Something about this place soothed her soul. Her physical wounds were healing and would be gone soon. The emotional scars, of course, would take longer.

After a bit, she heard footsteps approaching. "Hey, sweetheart, I need to show you something," Kane said from behind her.

She stood, accepted his hand, before he walked her toward the meadow. When he had her where he wanted her, he kissed her lips and then turned her toward the place he would build their home.

"Oh, Kane, it's perfect. We'll be able to see the creek from our porch."

"Hmm," he murmured happily. "I can picture standing on that porch, with your hand resting protectively over your growing belly."

Her head whipped around to see Kane kneeling on the ground with a red box in his hand. Her eyes burned with tears as she watched him.

"Annika, sweetheart. Will you marry me and become the best part of my life?"

"Yes," she answered, almost knocking him over with her hug.

"Never in a million years did I picture any of this, but from the moment I met you, what I wanted crystallized in my mind."

Kane grabbed her hand, slipping the perfectly sized ring onto her finger before moving her hand to cover his heart. Then he pulled her face to his and captured her lips in a soul-searing kiss. When he pulled back, he rested his head against her forehead.

Tears flowed down Annika's cheeks. "I do have one request, though. Before you break ground on our dream home, I want to make love to you right here in our meadow."

Kane's eyes darkened with desire. "It's a large piece of land, sweetheart. It might take a few attempts to properly christen our property."

"Deal!" She popped up and held her hand out to Kane. "Now, let's go share our news with Trent."

January—Current Day

Mill Creek

Annika smiled and pointed to Maggie. "Then we met you the next morning when you arrived unexpectedly."

"Oh, my God, that seems like a year ago instead of a measly six months," Maggie said. She wrapped Annika up in a hug. "Thank you for letting us into your heart."

Aimee came over next and joined in on the hug. "I'm so glad that dickhead is dead. You're fierce, girl."

"Me?" Annika narrowed her eyes. "I think you need to look in the mirror, Aimee. I survived yes, but you endured your entire world being ripped out from under you."

Jasmine refilled each champagne flute. "Wow, I'm speechless, Annika. Can I just say, I'm so grateful to call you badass women my friends."

Aimee raised her glass and waited until everyone followed. "Each of us went through hell to get where we are today. To the Goddess Warriors of Mill Creek."

They clinked and laughed together. Annika had the best girlfriends and the world's greatest husband a woman could ever want.

Turn the page for a sneak peak of Trent's Redemption, the first book in the Mill Creek Mystique series.

Have you read the romance that started the series?

Enjoy this sneak peek of

TRENT'S REDEMPTION

Book 1 in the Mill Creek Mystique romantic suspense series

Chapter One

THE RAPID KNOCK AT Trent's front door had him hoping that this unexpected interruption would spare him another lonely evening. Hastening his steps, he twisted the knob and sucked in a sharp breath. Nothing would have prepared him for this sight. His partner's sister and the woman he had dated. Margaret King's haunted green eyes stared back at him. Her blonde hair was thrown into a loose ponytail. Several strands had escaped and fluttered in the evening breeze. Even disheveled, she was still beautiful.

Dread settled in his gut, anchoring a weight to his chest as Dalton's last words filtered through his mind. *Promise me you'll look after her and keep her safe.*

"Maggie, what brings you here?" Trent's mind raced with possibilities, and none settled the growing dread that rotted in his stomach.

Her eyes widened briefly before she found her voice. "Can I come inside?"

"Of course, sorry," he stammered, moving aside and making a sweeping motion with his arm.

She hesitated for a second, then looked over her shoulder toward the driveway. Turning back, she met his gaze and released a deep breath. Remorse slapped him in the face as she entered his home. The last time he'd seen her was about ten months ago at Dalton's funeral. Not once had Trent reached out to see how she had adjusted to life without her brother. Now, the weight of his mistake stood in his entryway. Guilt riddled his body and his gaze shifted toward the floor because he'd let her down.

The subtle scent of oranges and vanilla floated by him as she passed. The moonlight shining through the open window cast a silvery glow across her pinched face. He clicked the deadbolt then flipped on the light before he sat on the sofa, waiting for her to join him. Her feet didn't budge, but her gaze circled the room.

Maggie raised an eyebrow, her eyes blank. "I'm sorry I didn't call first. I thought this discussion would be best in person. I can't believe I had to search the internet to find your address."

"I'm glad you're here, and I should have given you my address. There's no excuse for that..."

The tension in the room increased with every second of silence that followed.

"I-I don't know what to think anymore. You might think I'm crazy or worse, have overreacted to drive all the way here." Her voice sounded like sandpaper on wood.

Trent grabbed her hand and swiped his thumb softly across her knuckles. A rush of emotions flooded his system with that simple touch. He hated the strain emanating from her body. "Are you okay, Maggie?"

He released her hand and patted the spot next to him. The cushions dipped as she sat, her gaze lingering on the room and surroundings. "Why do you have scaffolding outside? Did something happen to your home?"

Trent smiled and shook his head. "No, I just finished renovating the interior and have decided to upgrade my roof. What's going on, Maggie?"

She turned to him, flashing a brief smile. "Good. I'm glad nothing bad happened to you. Could I have a glass of water?"

"You can have anything you'd like." He meant those words and vowed to himself to prove it to her. "But you need to tell me what's upset you. What made you drive all this way to find me?"

The single tear traveling down her cheek gutted him. Her resolve and strength may have had her sitting beside him, holding herself together, but her vulnerability undid him. He tugged her body against his, to feel her warmth and the pulse of her heart as he held her tight. To remind her she wasn't alone in dealing with whatever worried her. Even if his actions these last ten months told a different story.

A niggle of hope bloomed in his chest when she hugged him back just as fiercely. This wouldn't erase his absence from her life since the death of her brother, but maybe she'd see it as an olive branch to reconnect them to days long past. To the days when they were friends and all three of them spent time together.

When she sat back against the cushion, dark circles marred the delicate skin beneath her eyes. Trent's mind whirled with a million questions. Had someone hurt her? Had Maggie been with a man who threatened her? Why was she here? All of them remained unspoken because shame swamped his system. Not only was he a shitty person, but he'd broken a promise to his friend.

If only I'd taken out the shooter in the rafters, Dalton would still be here. Suffocated by the memories of that horrible day, Trent shot up off the sofa, desperately needing air and space. "I'll get you that water. When I return, how about you start from the beginning and explain why you're here? We'll figure this out together."

"Thanks. You're the one person I knew would understand," she said in a mere whisper.

Jesus, what had she been through that would make her run? The woman he'd known was full mirth and energy. He hated the mixture of defeat and uncertainty radiating from the depths of her green eyes.

"Here you go, Miss Margaret King." Trent handed her a glass of water.

"Ugh, call me Maggie, you know better. My parents called me Margaret, and that was when I was in trouble." She stared into the distance for a moment. "Maggie Moo was the nickname my brother preferred," she added with a slight wobble in her voice. "Sorry, I miss him so much. I just never thought I'd lose him after my parents died. I figured we'd grow old together. It's been difficult knowing I'm all alone in the world."

Trent's heart was clogged with condemnation. "Never apologize for missing him. Dalton loved you. He would've done anything for you. You were his little sister. Hell, I'd known him since training at Quantico, and I knew then, he'd be the biggest pain in my ass and best friend. His death left a hole in our lives." The words he left unspoken were that he'd abandoned her, too.

A soft giggle escaped her lips. "Yes, he could be a pain. He also tried controlling my life down to who I dated."

Trent nodded in agreement. "Yes, he had firm opinions on who should date you and why."

"If I recall, you did, too, since you cited your job as a complication of our relationship. Anyway, blood or not, you've always been a part of my family, which is why I'm here." She forced a slow steady stream of air into her lungs. "You were both logical and rational men who worked from facts to solve life's problems. I've lost count of how often I've endured a lecture about being observant and always aware of my surroundings."

He interjected, "A smart person assessed their situation and acted accordingly. That coincidences rarely, if ever, exist. Yes, I speak that same dialect."

"You are cut from the same cloth as Dalton, which is why I'm in Mill Creek. I've analyzed my situation and my findings have shocked me." She gulped the cool liquid. Straightening her spine, she continued, "Dalton made me promise—almost to the point of ritualistic chanting—that if I were ever in trouble and couldn't reach him, I should call you. I always thought he'd meant while he was alive..." Tears streamed down her face. "I think someone has been following me because I'm Dalton's sister."

Trent's eyes narrowed. She'd piqued his curiosity with that assessment. He then schooled his features so they'd remain neutral. "Why would you think that?"

"At first, I noticed a white van parked on the street facing my apartment. It appeared after Dalton's death. The days and times were random, but it was the same van. It disappeared for a while, then returned a few weeks ago. I can't explain it, but I got a strange feeling about it."

Maggie fidgeted, cracking her fingers one by one. He sat quietly while she fidgeted with nervous energy. He didn't want to add to her stress, so he gave her the time she needed to process her thoughts.

"How? What made it seem unusual?"

She lifted her gaze to meet his eyes and shrugged. "I only saw the driver and passenger twice, but I'm pretty sure they were the same men from the first time. This sounds crazy, I know it does, which is why I didn't report the van to the police. Those men could have lived in the complex or in the area. What happened the other night changed my mind, but instead of calling the police, I headed straight to you. This is personal, Trent, and it scared me."

"I'm glad you came to me." He gently urged her to continue by nodding and keeping his expression neutral. Deep down, his stomach knotted with apprehension over what came next.

A tiny smile crossed her lips. "God, you remind me of him, fierce and protective. I appreciate that you're not judging me—at least until I'm done."

"You're doing just fine, now, keep going."

"Early Saturday morning, I was working at my computer when the fire alarms went off. When I went outside to check, the adjacent unit had smoke billowing from inside. My neighbor appeared outside with her child, panicked, and talking into the phone about a grease fire and firemen coming. I ducked back inside my place to retrieve my messenger bag, which held everything that mattered to me and waited outside with my neighbor. After the firemen arrived and controlled the scene, I was informed that the fire was out, but it would be a couple of hours before I could return. I decided to head to our local coffee shop to hang out while the chaos passed. When I returned..."

The color drained from her cheeks. She lowered her head to stare at the carpet between her feet. "My front door was ajar, again, which I figured was so the firemen could finish their investigation. I caught a glimpse of that white van pulling away. When I entered, everything seemed fine...until I reached my office. Drawers were opened with papers and folders scattered across my desk and floor. Then, I noticed a knife stabbed into my desk holding a note that read, 'What did he know?'"

Trent snapped his brows together, his mouth drawn tight. He couldn't quell his reaction to what he'd just heard. The hairs on his neck bristled. He didn't know how, but he'd find a way to slay each and every one of her demons...or die trying. He owed Dalton that much.

"Why didn't you call the police? Do you know if anything was taken? Were other rooms searched?" Trent squeezed her hand a few times, bringing her gaze upward.

With her other hand, she reached for the glass and gulped the last few sips before she answered, "In my gut, I know this reaches beyond the police. The only 'he' in my life was my brother. My brain went into survival mode. I had to get out of my apartment and get to you. You'd know what to do. I-I didn't look any further. All I kept thinking was, this can't be good to have a knife stabbed into your desk, especially with how he died. I took my bag, hit the bank, and withdrew as much money as allowed. I left my car at the office and called a car rental company. I decided leaving my car behind was best. I stopped at one truck stop to rest, used only cash, then drove until I pulled into your driveway."

She sat still as if she had waited for him to say something. Processing what he had just heard shredded his insides. The last time they had spoken was at the funeral, and that encounter was strained, not ugly or mean, just distant because of him. This was opposite to how he and Maggie usually interacted. Instead, he struggled with his anger and self-condemnation while nursing the injuries he'd sustained that day alongside Dalton. As a result, Trent's job and assignment changed, which deprived him of retribution. He hated the exhaustion etched across her face. Starting now, he would atone for his wrongs.

"Brave and resilient is what you are." A surge of pride and respect flood his system. "You did damn good with disappearing off the grid and adapting in the face of adversity. You're far from an agent but acted cautiously and logically."

Fatigue, stress, and fear radiated from her, but he also saw a brief glimmer of relief. That was something he would build upon.

"Your brother would be proud. Hell, I'm proud of you. I'm also so damn sorry I haven't reached out before now. I own that. My apology doesn't change anything, but I hope my actions will. *If* you give me that chance. I'd say you read the situation right—a clusterfuck for sure."

Her eyes closed for a moment, and her shoulders dipped as tension seemed to fade from her body. Something deep inside Trent's stomach twisted painfully. Had she thought he might deny her his support and protection? Of course, why wouldn't she? It wasn't his intent, but he'd basically removed her from his life. Another epic screw-up to add to his list that he needed to fix.

He cupped her chin. "I understand why you weren't sure about coming to me for help, so I'll clarify that misconception now. I will always protect you, Maggie. You have my word."

She shifted her head from his grasp and stabbed him in the chest with a finger. "You hurt my feelings, but I'm not blameless either. You have to promise you won't put yourself in jeopardy in any way. I can't stand the thought of losing another person."

The painful truth behind those words constricted his chest. The vibrant woman he had known seemed to have retreated somewhat. Trent snatched her hand, loving how buttery soft her skin was under his fingertips. "Give me your keys. I think it's best to put your rental in the garage for now."

She stood and dug into her front pocket to retrieve the key ring. "Thanks for allowing me into your home, especially with my trouble in tow."

Trent extended his palm and caught the keys. "You always were trouble. I'll give you the grand tour first and point out the highlights from my renovation."

"I thought you liked living out of boxes. You know, afraid of commitment."

"Smart ass," he lamented. "I'm working on unpacking everything."

He couldn't imagine what she thought when she arrived but was glad she'd come. He started in his kitchen, explaining how his friend Kane had updated everything to stainless and gas.

"This is amazing. I love the gas stovetop. That refrigerator must keep you fed for months. It's huge."

"I've heard that bigger is always better," he deadpanned.

She rolled her eyes and protested, "Seriously? You haven't changed one bit."

He flashed her an exaggerated wink and guided her through the rest of the house. When they reached the master bathroom, he showed her his second favorite feature from the renovation: his walk-in shower with multiple adjusting heads that also produced steam. He owed Kane for this gem, too. Her small whimper when she spied the shower didn't go unnoticed. Trent also hadn't missed how closely she followed him the entire time. He'd do anything to diminish the worry radiating from her body. He ended his tour with the room she'd be using and the bathroom.

At the door to the bathroom, he paused and met her eyes. "Why don't you shower in my bathroom while I move the vehicle? You can give me a woman's perspective on my shower."

She leaned her head against the doorway and sighed. "A shower sounds heavenly, but I'll use the guest bath. Will you grab my bag from the front room and put it on the bed?

"Sure, do you have anything in the caryou need?"

Her mouth twisted into a frown. "No, I didn't pack any clothing or even think about bringing my bathroom supplies. In my haste, I went with the less is more theory. Do you have a toothbrush and paste? And if I could borrow a few things to wear, that would be super. Walking around naked might be kind of awkward."

He groaned internally as his mind conjured several inappropriate scenarios involving her sans clothing. Built like a goddess, with her curves and creamy skin, he'd love nothing more than to see her naked. He caught her staring at his reflection in the bathroom mirror and knew he'd been nailed. His traitorous cock stirred behind the confines of his pants. This woman still caused his mind and body to want more from her. Definitely his cue to leave.

"I'll put a T-shirt and a pair of sweatpants on your bed. Leave your clothes outside the door, I'll wash them for you. We'll go shopping tomorrow to fill in whatever else you left behind."

She opened her mouth as if to speak, then clamped her lips together as she moved into the bathroom.

"What's on your mind?" he asked.

"Do you have any cereal or yogurt? Something easy to fix."

He put both hands on his waist and cocked one eyebrow. "You can have whatever you want. When did you eat last?"

Her eyes narrowed, and her mouth gaped. "I-ah, a granola at the truck stop."

He shook his head. "You're my priority. That includes food, sleep, protection, and whatever else I've forgotten to mention. Get that through your thick, stubborn, and beautiful head." Trent punctuated his point by wrapping her in a crushing hug. He wasn't sure what else to do, a move so familiar from all the previous times he and Dalton had visited between assignments or while on break.

He sighed as her curves melded perfectly against his frame and in all the right places. A surge of possessiveness roared to life within him, and not only did it startle him, but it also made him back away, breaking their connection

"Shower, then kitchen," he said in a tone that encouraged no debate.

He headed down the hall and heard the snick of the door as it closed behind him. Needing to put space between them, he'd take care of her car. This woman in his home was Dalton's sister. The same baby sister his partner proclaimed off limits to any man who worked in a risky profession. Dalton was adamant that Maggie should marry a man with a stable job, allowing him to come home every night. A man whose existence wasn't nestled in danger, with the potential to cause her harm because his job encompassed every aspect of his life. Trent had squashed his attraction to her because he hadn't wanted to ruffle Dalton's feathers. Even though he hadn't been exempt from Dalton's censure, he had to agree with the man. She deserved better. She deserved a marriage where her husband would be around every damn night. Whose job wouldn't risk her safety or threaten their lives. A fact of his employment he couldn't offer.

~ * ~

Relief washed over Maggie's body the moment Trent agreed with her assessment. That she hadn't overreacted. She never should have doubted that he'd support her, but hearing it from his lips alleviated her apprehension. The warmth from his embrace grounded her. If she could press the rewind button, she'd rather go back to when Trent held her in his arms. There was a familiarity to it, and she'd missed the simplicity of knowing someone had her back.

She'd gotten to know him when she went to college in Washington, D.C. and had chosen to live in Dalton's place instead of on campus. Her brother brought Trent home during break when they were both at Quantico. Not only had they become partners but friends. It wasn't like he was home often with his career, but it gave her an excuse to be close to her brother. She and Trent had dated a few times, but he had ended saying he didn't have time for a relationship due to his career. Her brother would never answer her question, but she would put money down on the fact he interfered.

When Trent smiled and flashed the bluest eyes she'd ever seen, it could melt the panties right off a girl. Never in her life had she experienced such a strong reaction to another person. It also didn't hurt that he was devastatingly gorgeous at six feet tall with his athletic build and all those well-defined muscles. His touch still made her girly parts tingle.

She'd cranked the shower tap to the left. When the bathroom mirror fogged over from the steam, she tugged back the curtain, adjusted the heat, then stepped inside. The hot spray pulsed against her tired muscles and sluiced down her body. She visualized removing Trent's shirt off his body to reveal raised pectorals and a ripped abdomen that flowed into a trim waist with sculpted hips. She bit her bottom lip and moaned. Well, that was what happened when one was sex deprived and surrounded by male hotness.

She adjusted the dial until a cold blast of water jolted her system. That daydream would be her little secret. She needed to stop this line of thinking. He probably had a bevy of beautiful women on speed dial. The type who looked perfect even after a torrential rainstorm. The exact same type her brother had circling him at all times. A girl could dream, couldn't she?

After stepping from the shower, she dried off and slathered on some lotion she found in the cabinet. She finger-combed her hair and mentally added an actual one to her list of things to buy. There was nothing like a shower to make a person feel human again. Towel wrapped around her body, she padded to the bedroom he assigned. As promised, sitting on her bed were the clothes and the items from her car. She removed a stuffed animal from her tote and kissed the cow on its nose before putting it back inside. She'd give anything to hear Dalton call her by her nickname one more time.

As she made her way to the kitchen, she took in his home. It had the perfect blend of cabin and modern.

The center of the room had a wooden dining table with four chairs, and in front of one chair sat a grilled cheese sandwich, her absolute favorite. Especially when she was having a crappy day.

Trent looked over his shoulder holding a spoon. "You look more relaxed. The tomato soup will be ready in a minute. These are my go-to choices when I need comfort food."

Her insides melted like the cheese in the sandwich.

"Mine too," she said. The part she kept to herself watching a hot man cook for her did wicked things to her body. Good grief, she needed to get a grip. He was being nice, not offering her a night of decadent sex. Or a life of love, marriage, and children. The fantasy train needed to stop so she could disembark because that destination did not exist.

The last few months had changed her. She had to find a way to survive before her grief and despair consumed her entirely. Being around Trent has created a few sparks in the recesses of her mind, reminding her of the woman she had been and what they had shared.

"Are you for real? A good-looking man who can cook and isn't afraid to admit that grilled cheese and tomato soup have the power to cure most things in life. I think I've died and gone to heaven," she tossed out and took a seat at the table.

He rolled his eyes and huffed dramatically. "I hate to burst your bubble, but men can do many things these days. I can even load the dishwasher and do laundry, but I draw the line at ironing."

Maggie burst out laughing. "Ah, I needed that. It's been a while."

Trent ladled soup into a bowl. "Feel free to laugh anytime. It suits you very nicely. I also happen to appreciate the eye candy comment."

Did he just flirt with her? She took a bite of her sandwich and moaned. "This is delicious."

"The secret is mayonnaise instead of butter. It's how my mom makes them. Tonight, I want you to promise me you'll rest. I don't like seeing those dark circles under your eyes."

"I'll try, but it's hard to get my brain to stop churning over everything." She blew on a spoonful of soup.

"Well, I promise to keep the boogie men away. Hey, one question, though. Something you said earlier confused me. You said you left your car at the office. Do schoolteachers refer to their classrooms as offices now? Are you still teaching?"

She put down her spoon. "No. I quit teaching."

His eyebrows knit together as he processed what she said, but to her relief, he didn't question her any further. She didn't want to get into it tonight. Her love of teaching had died after she buried Dalton. The burden of life's truths wore her down, and she couldn't handle deceiving those precious faces daily.

Trent filled in the prolonged silence. "We can talk about all of this tomorrow after you get some rest."

"Okay," she said between a spoonful of soup.

"Oh, one more thing. I'm meeting some friends for breakfast tomorrow. I want you to come. Afterward, we'll head to the store to pick up whatever else you need."

Maggie took a big gulp of water. "I don't want to impose."

"I see your listening skills haven't improved," he muttered sardonically. "We're meeting them tomorrow at eight. I'll have your clothes folded and waiting for you outside your door. You'll love the Knotty Pine Tree. The food is delicious, and I want you to meet my friends,

Kane and Annika. They're good people; you can trust them. Besides, your smart actions put distance between what happened in Dallas and what happened here. It'll give us some time to figure it all out."

There was a time when meeting new people and being a social butterfly came naturally, but that part of her died when she put Dalton in the ground. Maybe she should label her life accordingly now. BD—before Dalton—and AD—after Dalton.

The scaffolding outside the kitchen window reminded her of a skeleton in the moonlight. She hated the nights the most. All her fears and problems grew into large, creepy monsters that caused her constant worry that whoever left the note would find her.

Trent's Redemption, Book 1 in the Mill Creek Mystique romantic suspense series is out now.

Acknowledgements

The writing world is, for the most part, a solitary space. Still, I've been fortunate to connect with many amazing, talented people who share a passion for bringing heartfelt stories to the world. I've also made exceptional friends along the way. The laughter, tears, and lessons from our interactions are priceless. I'm honored to have found these individuals, along with friends who have unconditionally supported me on my journey.

Living in the fantasyland of happily-ever-afters is one of my favorite pastimes. The things I've learned through research, blended with my imagination and the experiences I've had or the outcomes I wish had been different in my life, give me the foundation to develop all kinds of adventures and escapades. The best part is that I get to control the outcomes.

Speaking of great support, brainstorming, feedback, and everything in between, I want to personally recognize a few individuals whose unconditional love and support mean the world to me. Jordanne, for your detailed insight and feedback. I love having you in my corner! A Fabulous Production has been my go-to resource for social media formatting, layout, and graphics. I can always count on you for anything. Cindy, your energy and sarcasm are infectious. I can always count on you to make me smile! To DL, whose unwavering support in all things continually challenges me to reach for the stars! I adore you!

My Vicki Jean, thanks for reading to me every night when I was little! You were my kick-start to becoming an author. And to my ride-or-die, my infinity and beyond, life with you is never dull. It's filled with adventure and laughter, and if I ever got a do-over, you'd be a no-brainer.

A huge thank you to my ARC Stars. I appreciate your willingness and time spent reading my story and providing your insightful feedback and reviews. You are amazing, and I'm honored to have you on my team.

Lastly, but never least, thank you to my fantastic Readers who chose to read this book. I hope Kane and Annika's story gave you a brief escape from reality, an adventure that left you smiling and your heart filled with love.

I greatly appreciate your support!

XOXO,

Bailey

BOOKS BY BAILEY THOMAS

ROMANTIC SUSPENSE

Mill Creek Mystique Series

Trent's Redemption
Hidden Identities
Breaking Point
Kane's Reckoning
Legally Bound (Coming Soon)

Available in Audio

Available in Audio

Available in Audio

CONTEMPORARY ROMANCE

Sand Dollars, Secrets, and Starting Over

Part of the Love in Destiny romance series

Torrent of Hearts

Also available in the Pack Your Bags short story collection

Amazon Top Ten author Bailey Thomas writes romantic suspense, contemporary, and adventure romance, and she loves a well-earned happily-ever-after.

As an only child, she was always kept busy by her active imagination and adventurous spirit. Now, she channels her creativity into romantic adventures. A sucker for heroes and heroines with big hearts, baggage, and the fight to overcome life's challenges and earn their HEA.

She lives in the beautiful yet hot Southwest. When she's not working on her next deadline at a computer, she's reading, traveling, or watching sports. Life is too short, so Bailey lives by her motto of seeking adventures that bring her joy.

She loves hearing from readers. For more details about her books, appearances, and adventures, you can find her and connect with her at the links below.

Website/Blog:

baileythomasauthor.com

Instagram

instagram.com/Author_BaileyThomas

BookBub

bookbub.com/authors/bailey-thomas

www.ingramcontent.com/pod-product-compliance
Lightning Source LLC
La Vergne TN
LVHW091043080826
845145LV00002B/600